The kids at  have a lot on their minds:

Blake: "I just don't understand why everyone wants to get so tied down. Kids already have school and parents on their backs. Who needs to complicate things by falling in love? And why would Rainey go for a guy like Tucker? Why?"

Rainey: "All I seem to think about is how to get my dad safely out of town. But Tucker seems so removed from my problems . . . always carefree and just perpetually lucky. I can admire a guy like that."

Tucker: "It's good to be back at West Mount after private school. And the best thing is the girls. That Rainey is . . . interesting. Rumor has it Blake has a real case for her. Not that that has anything to do with Rainey and me."

Susan: "Jesse just doesn't understand. My dad's crazy on the subject of Jesse's family. If I tell him I'm in love with *that boy*, he'll scream until my hair turns gray. And I *still* won't be allowed to see Jesse."

Jesse: "I love Susan, but this sneaking around is driving me nuts. And what happens when her dad finds out she's been seeing me behind his back? Because sooner or later, he will."

Books by Janice Harrell

EASY ANSWERS
WILD TIMES AT WEST MOUNT HIGH

Available from ARCHWAY Paperbacks

Easy
ANSWERS

Janice Harrell

AN ARCHWAY PAPERBACK
Published by POCKET BOOKS
New York   London   Toronto   Sydney   Tokyo   Singapore

This book is a work of fiction. Names, characters, places and incidents are either the product of the author's imagination or are used fictitiously. Any resemblance to actual events or locales or persons, living or dead, is entirely coincidental.

AN ARCHWAY PAPERBACK *Original*

An Archway Paperback published by
POCKET BOOKS, a division of Simon & Schuster Inc.
1230 Avenue of the Americas, New York, NY 10020

ISBN: 0-671-68571-6

First Archway Paperback printing March 1990

10 9 8 7 6 5 4 3 2 1

AN ARCHWAY PAPERBACK and colophon are
registered trademarks of Simon & Schuster Inc.

Printed in the U.S.A.

IL 6+

ONE

*J*unior year. It should be a good year for falling in love and for taking the SAT, and Rainey Locklear planned on doing both. But what she hadn't counted on was the trapped feeling that had swept over her and made her goals seem irrelevant. It was February and the bleak gray sky made the brick walls of West Mount High look like those of a prison. Suddenly what she craved most was a ticket out of town.

She signed her name in bold strokes to the sheet on the covered bulletin board outside under the sign "Science Club: Overnight trip to the Museum of Natural History, Washington, D.C." She hated buses and here she was signing up for ten hours on one. She had to be crazy. Worse, nobody she knew was even going.

"You doing that?" Blake Farraby leaned against the administration building.

"It'll be fun." Rainey shot him a hopeful look. "Why don't you come, too, Blake?"

He shook his head. "Nah. I won't be here that weekend. We're taking off a couple of extra days and flying up to Canada to do some skiing."

Usually Rainey made it a point not to waste energy on things that couldn't be helped, but the winter had undermined this sensible resolve. She found herself wishing she were rich, wishing she were tall, and most immediately, wishing Blake would go on the Washington trip. She scuffed her shoe restlessly against the sidewalk and stared at the list. "I just wish somebody I knew was going."

"It'll probably be mostly sophomores. You're going to get pretty tired of hearing them sing 'Ninety-nine Bottles of Beer on the Wall.' "

"I know, but I've just got to get away from this place. I'm starting to go bonkers."

"Maybe you can get Ann Lee to go. It's her kind of thing. You know, educational and chaperoned."

"I already asked her. She's got an interview that weekend for some special summer abroad thing."

"No kidding. Hey, how about Michael? Nah, I guess not. He's pretty tied up these days."

"Everybody's pretty tied up but me. My life is dull, empty, and very possibly meaningless. I've got to get away from here." An icy drop of water fell on the bridge of her nose like a punctuation to her complaint. She wiped a mitten across her nose. "I ab dot a winter person!" She sneezed emphatically.

The violent ringing of the bell set three thousand kids in motion and soon Blake was swept away from Rainey by the traffic. She had the sensation she had been just about to ask him something, but she couldn't remember what it was. Her

2

mind was moving more and more slowly every day, as if she were running on solar batteries and winding down. There was no question that she needed to get away. Her first choice would have been a week on a Caribbean island, but that was out of the question. There was little cash at her house for extras. Her father, a Lumbee Indian activist, had disappeared three years earlier after taking hostages at gunpoint in an attempt to publicize his cause. His rare messages home contained no return address, much less any money to help out.

Rainey didn't kid herself about the trip to the Museum of Natural History. It wasn't the same as a trip to the sunny beaches of the Caribbean. Still, it had its charms. And she had never been to Washington so it would, at least, be different.

At midday, when Rainey saw Susan Brantley just ahead of her in the lunch line, she decided her life was not ready to take a turn for the better. Susan's heart-shaped face was surrounded by a mass of crimped blond hair, and as she tilted her head to listen to Ann Lee Smith talk, she absently tapped a fingernail on her perfect white front teeth. Her nails were lavender and on every finger she wore a gold ring.

What Rainey hated about Susan was that all the best things fell into her lap. True love. Funds for college. An unlimited number of gold rings. Rainey felt in no mood to be mature about it.

Ann Lee was speaking earnestly. "This is my chance! I've got it all figured out." Ann Lee and Susan were best friends, something that still surprised Rainey a little. It didn't seem like the most obvious pairing—the goody-goody and the princess.

Susan frowned at Ann Lee. "But are you sure you're ready to give up burgers and fries for that long?"

"Don't you see, I'm stagnating!" Ann Lee sniffled and dabbed at her raw-looking pink nose. "Intellectually and emotionally, there's nothing new here for me anymore. If I could live with a family in some foreign country and learn about the country from inside, it would extremely educational."

With a jolt Rainey recognized an echo of her own desperate desire to get away. "What country are you interested in?" she asked.

"Any country. I'm not particular."

"You're really that desperate, huh?" said Susan.

"Why should you be surprised that I want to travel? I guess you think I'm such a stick-in-the-mud I could never want to do anything that was at all interesting. That's it, isn't it?"

"No, no," Susan said hastily. "It's just that, gee, you've never even been away from home before and going away to another country seems like, well, an awful big way for you to start off, that's all."

Blake touched Rainey on the arm. "Hey, guys. Can I butt in line?"

No one behind the three girls protested when Blake cut in line. Because of his Corvette, his status as a junior, and, most importantly, his reputation as a nice guy, Blake could cut in front of half the people in the school if he wanted to. That was the way the pecking order worked at West Mount High. "You need a vacation. I see the signs," he told Ann Lee.

"I need something, all right," she said and sighed.

Susan adjusted the lavender ribbon that almost contained the wildness of her crimped hair. "I guess I haven't mentioned it. I couldn't quite make up my mind at first, but I applied for that exchange program, too."

Ann Lee stiffened. "You *what*?"

"Applied for that program. I know they only take a few people, but a friend of my mother's is on the board and she said she'd recommend me."

"I thought that's what you said." Ann Lee tried a little smile, but it didn't quite come off.

"It's kind of a shot in the dark, but I thought I'd give it a try and see what happens."

"A summer is a long, long time," said Ann Lee quickly. "What if Jesse gets lonely and starts going with somebody else?"

"Oh, he's going to work for his uncle this summer. If I'm here I'd just have to sit around by myself a lot. So I figure why not do something? Mrs. Harkness told me she wrote me a super recommendation." Susan grinned. "She said I had a sparkling and charismatic personality and that I had the best ear for foreign languages of any student she had had in a decade. How about that for laying it on?"

Ann Lee looked faintly ill. Rainey could understand her feelings perfectly.

"Maybe we'll both end up going," Susan said. "Wouldn't that be cool?"

Ann Lee and Susan hadn't been eating lunch together for a while because Susan ate lunch with her boyfriend, Jesse McCracken, every day. So when Rainey carried her tray to a table by the window, Ann Lee followed her.

"I just know Susan's going to get picked for it instead of me." Ann Lee banged her tray on the table.

"I don't know why you say that. I'll bet you've got better grades."

"Grades are not what they're looking for. They want somebody who is, and I quote, 'outgoing, friendly, adaptable, and a good representative of the United States.' That's

Susan, right? And now it turns out her mom has a friend on the board on top of it."

"Oh, come on. You never can tell how it's going to go."

"I can tell all right. At my fifth birthday party we played pin the tail on the donkey, and I actually ended up getting the booby prize. At my own birthday party. The pattern was set very early. I don't win these things."

"If you're so sure about that, why don't you skip the interview and go on the trip to D.C.? It'd be fun."

"Oh, no, I keep going through the motions, coming in second, being a good sport. It's my fate. Susan was born to be a star, and I was born to be a good sport."

Rainey lifted the cheese off her burger and slapped it down on her plate. "I don't believe in fate."

"But you've got to! Look around you. What about Susan and Jesse?" Ann Lee blew her nose and peeked over her handful of tissue toward the east corner where Susan and Jesse were sitting. "Look at them. They aren't even eating. Don't you see how they were made for each other? They're like Romeo and Juliet."

"If Susan's dad finds out it's going to be more like *The Day After*."

"You just aren't a romantic, are you, Rainey?"

"That's not true. I am a romantic. Only I figure romance, like everything else, is out there for anybody who has enough initiative to go after it."

"But that doesn't make any sense. You can't just decide to fall in love."

"I don't see why not."

Ann Lee smiled. "I just hope I'm there to see it when you fall in love."

"Maybe you will be," said Rainey. She knew better than to invite derision by telling Ann Lee she had decided to fall in love sometime soon. Of course, she didn't know with whom yet. She hoped the answer to that question would come to her once her brain started functioning properly.

Just then Blake put his tray down on the table. Ann Lee sneezed juicily in his direction.

He drew back. "Jeez, do you have to come to school and give that cold to everybody?" Seeing that Ann Lee's eyes were shiny with tears, he added hastily, "Let me rephrase that. You ought to be home taking care of yourself and drinking hot chicken soup."

Ann Lee threw her napkin on her plate and got up. "You're right." Her voice quavered. "I'm going to go sign out."

Blake watched her retreating back. "I guess I said the wrong thing, huh?"

"That's not it." Rainey opened her milk container with such an abrupt motion that milk spurted out. "She's really down about competing with Susan for that exchange program thing. She's already decided she's going to lose. Talk about defeatist—she doesn't have a particle of self-confidence."

Blake sat down. "I guess you wouldn't know about that, huh?"

"Okay, I don't understand why she puts herself down. So, sue me." Rainey realized that in her current fragile state of mind she simply could not tolerate Ann Lee's despair. She almost had the feeling it might be catching. She looked around. "Where's Michael? He's not with you?"

He's over at the hospital having lunch with his lady, the nurse."

"You mean he just takes off and goes over there? Is that legal?"

"Have you ever known Michael to worry about legal?"

7

The old gang is sort of breaking up, isn't it? It used to be Michael and Susan ate lunch with the rest of us.''

"That was just because we used to have that assigned seating. It's not as if we were all such close friends or anything.''

"Is that some kind of delicate hint, Rainey? You want me to shove off? Is that it?''

She looked at him in amazement. "Good grief! Everybody is so touchy today!''

Blake shrugged. "Okay, I'm touchy. It's getting on my nerves. Michael and I used to have a lot of laughs, but now he spends all his time with this perfect stranger. And look at Susan and Jesse.'' He glanced at them. "Okay, don't look at Susan and Jesse. I'll admit it's embarrassing.''

"Ann Lee says it's fate.''

"It's stupid. Why do sane people suddenly go out of their minds? Michael's been babbling on about this nurse for months now. I tell you, it wouldn't surprise me all that much if I woke up one day to find out he'd gotten married.''

"You're kidding, of course.''

"I'm not. Sure it would be a crazy thing to do, but when you think of it, *crazy* is kind of a one-word definition of Michael. Don't get me started. I can't understand it. I mean, he's got school tying him down already, right? And he's got his parents on his back. I mean, in the best case scenario, he's got that—minimum. So why does he want to tie himself down more? It's crazy. It's insane.'' He smoothed his dark hair with both hands. "I guess all this sounds pretty stupid, huh? Like if I could run everybody's life for them, it would be a lot better. I better get a grip or pretty soon I'll be sounding like my parents.''

"Nah.'' She smiled a little. "You're okay.'' Just a little stir-crazy, she thought. Like all the rest of us.

"You know what I'd like? I'd like to be in my Vette right now speeding down some highway to—"

"Katmandu?"

"I don't think they've got a highway to Katmandu. But somewhere far away, anyhow. With no strings attached."

"No chemistry test."

"That goes without saying."

"I just wish something would happen."

"Like a bomb threat."

Like love, thought Rainey.

TWO

_T_he following week Rainey stood outside the cafeteria at the Museum of Natural History wondering if she'd better skip lunch. She still felt sick from the five-hour bus ride and the endless choruses of "Ninety-nine Bottles of Beer." On the other hand, the bus had left West Mount High at six o'clock and the banana she had eaten for breakfast was a distant memory. There was a small chance she might faint if she didn't eat something. Maybe she'd better make herself eat whether she felt like it or not.

She glanced up at the tiger on the pediment. Frozen in full leap by the taxidermist, he had been dead for years, but he looked a lot better than she felt. The trip had not picked her up the way she had hoped.

"Rainey!"

A tall blond boy threw his arm around her and she was instantly crushed against a scratchy blue sweater.

She pulled away and looked up at him doubtfully. "Tucker?" Tucker Harbisson had grown a lot since she had last seen him, which was some time in the eighth grade. The flush of red across his nose and cheekbones suggested he had been spending a lot of time outdoors instead of studying, which fit with her memory of him.

"Is that all I get? How about a kiss?"

"Uh, w-what are you doing here?" she stuttered. "I thought you were at prep school."

"Right. I was. But Washington is 'away,' isn't it?"

"Is your class doing a field trip or something?"

"Nope. But Saint Anselm's is in Virginia and that's a suburb of D.C., practically. It's a short train ride from here."

"And they let you come into town anytime you want?"

"They think I'm having a lot of dental work done." He smiled broadly, revealing a perfect set of teeth. "I forged a note from my parents. While the school thinks I'm at the dentist, I take in a movie, eat some decent food for a change, and come by here to pick up beautiful girls. Let me buy you lunch. Not here. The food's better over at the art museum."

"But I can't just take off like that. I'm with a group from school."

He looked around. "Then how come I don't see people I know? Where is everybody?"

"Mostly sophomores came."

He made a face. "Well, have they got you chained at the ankles or something? Come on. Let's go."

He pulled her upstairs. When they stepped outside onto the Mall, wind blew her long dark hair across her face and the sudden chill took her breath away. "I hope nobody notices I'm gone."

"They won't. Taxi!"

Rainey never would have hailed a taxi to go such a short distance, but once she climbed in she had to admit it was good to get out of the cold and the wind. The taxi driver was annoyed at first, but he calmed down when they stopped in front of the art museum and Tucker tipped him ten dollars.

Tucker led her up the broad marble steps of the museum. Inside, there were tall white columns and big rooms lined with pictures.

"This is nice." Rainey looked around. "It's quieter than the natural history museum. I like it."

"We've got to be sure to get you back before your bus leaves," said Tucker. "When is that?"

"Not for a while yet." She didn't think it would be smart to tell him her group was spending the night at a hotel. She didn't want him shinnying up the balcony to her room and something told her he was perfectly capable of doing that.

They went downstairs to the museum cafeteria. At the entrance was a waterfall higher than her head. She gazed at the silvery sheet of water, fascinated. Droplets from the falling water bounced on the metal drain, dampening the terrazzo floor and the potted plants at its base. It seemed splendid to her that such sunlight, greenery, and glittering water could exist in an underground hallway.

When she and Tucker went through the cafeteria line, she was surprised at how much food she was putting on her tray. Her appetite had miraculously returned. They set their trays on a table and, sitting down, Rainey surveyed the room. At the next table a girl in a black leather miniskirt with spiked black hair was sharing a plate with a pale young man wearing suspenders and baggy pants. Nearby, a well-dressed matron tore open a packet of artificial sweetener and poured it into her tea while the schoolboys accompanying her blew at each other through their straws. It was a more sophisticated-looking bunch of people than Rainey normally saw at the mall at home and in their slightly exotic clothes they seemed to her to be extras in a movie—not real people with real lives.

"Trade you some french fries for some mousse and bread," Tucker said.

"Don't you want to get your own bread?"

"And get in that line again? No, thanks."

Rainey couldn't see the waterfall from where she was, but she could hear the falling water over the hum of voices in the cafeteria. It was hard for her to define the comforting quality of the sound, but its spell was almost hypnotic. It seemed to say that she could let go, that she didn't need to try so hard.

"This is nice," she said and sighed. "I'm glad we came."

"Is it the waterfall you like or my charming company?"

"Both, I guess."

"You're in luck," he chortled. He leaned back perilously far in his chair and threw out an arm in a wide gesture. "I'm coming back to West Mount High."

Rainey was startled. "What? On the bus?"

"No, of course not, dope. I mean, I'm transferring back. My parents are coming to pick me up tomorrow."

"What happened? Did Saint Anselm's throw you out?"

"Come on, do I look like the kind of guy who gets caught?"

"No, I guess not." Actually, he reminded her a lot of Susan. Maybe it was the perfect teeth.

"I'm just sick of being out in the boondocks with a bunch of other guys and a handful of prissy teachers. I don't know—it came over me all of a sudden. I've just had it. I'm fed up. Know what I mean?"

Rainey nodded. "Yup, I have some kind of idea."

"The place ain't cheap, either, so when I told my dad I was ready to come home, I didn't get a lot of arguments. The only thing is I'm out of touch with what's going on at home. It'll be practically like coming in new. I want you to fill me in some."

Now she understood why he had swooped down on her. She and Tucker might not have been exactly buddies back in the eighth grade, but currently his old friends weren't on the spot and she was.

"What do you want to know? I'm not even sure which kids you knew when you were at home."

"Start with Susan Brantley. What she's up to these days?"

"Very tight with Jesse McCracken. I think you can forget her. You want to know what girls are available? Is that it?"

"Nah. You're getting the wrong idea, Rainey. I've just got general, all-purpose curiosity."

"They've added AP English as an option, and it looks like they're finally going to get the new football stadium built."

"Hey, not *that* kind of curious. Just fill me in on the people, okay?"

"Blake Farraby got a red Corvette for his birthday."

"No joke. A Corvette, huh?" He looked slightly downcast.

"It's hard for me to do this, Tucker. I don't know what you're interested in."

"Everything. Tell me everything."

"I think you better wait until you get back. That's the best thing."

"What do you hear from you father?"

The question caught her off guard. "Nothing," she said blankly. "What did you think?"

"Sorry. I didn't realize it was a touchy subject."

"It's not a touchy subject." She looked down at her plate. It was as if a spotlight were shining on her face. Suddenly she felt hot and conspicuous.

"Just before I went away to school there were these screaming headlines everywhere, but I never found out how it turned out."

Probably he had forgotten all about it until he saw her, she thought. If he had really been interested he could have asked his parents or checked with somebody when he was home. She prodded her salad with her fork. "Basically, you were there when he jumped bail, I guess."

He nodded.

"So that's all there is to it. He took off and nobody has heard from him since." This was not strictly true since Rainey knew her father had called her aunt once or twice, and she herself had gotten a few brief unsatisfactory letters from him. A typical one had read "Niagara Falls is fantastic. Saw a little girl who reminded me a lot of you. Miss you, sweetheart, Love, Pappa." She had a small collection of his letters at the bottom of her bureau.

Tucker shook his head. "That's tough," he said. "I always thought he was a hero. Fighting for the rights of his people and all."

Rainey cut her meat carefully, as if she were dissecting it. "Yours is a minority view."

"You don't look at it that way?"

"I don't think about it much," she lied. "It all happened a long time ago."

"And all this time he's been on the lam. It's incredible. Like a movie or something. It's kind of neat. I've always thought I might like being an outlaw myself. You know, wear dark glasses, maybe grow a beard—alert every minute, life on the edge.''

Rainey almost wondered if Tucker was wired for sound, he was so interested in her father. Was it remotely possible that the FBI had enlisted the help of someone like Tucker? Her heart quickened for a second, but then she took a deep breath, and calm reason returned. Nah! It just couldn't be. She reminded herself that it had been three years since her father had dropped out of sight. He wasn't exactly the FBI's hottest case.

''I really don't know much about it.''

''Sorry, I didn't mean to be nosy. Am I making you uncomfortable?''

''No.''

''Because I just wanted to catch up on news and everything. I'm not trying to drive you up the wall.''

Recognizing this as the truth, she felt relief seep into her. She'd let the fantasy about the FBI run away with her for a minute.

''So, tell me why nobody came on this trip but you.''

Rainey exhaled. ''I guess they all just had better things to do. Michael—you remember Michael Dessaseaux—these days he's never separated from this nurse he's going with. Then Susan Brantley and Ann Lee Smith had to go to an interview for some summer abroad program, and Blake is skiing in Canada.''

He raised his eyebrows. ''Is that the crowd you hang out with these days?''

''Oh, I don't know. I guess so. Sort of.''

''I'm going to be starting all over. All those cliques. Brr,'' he shuddered. ''I'll have to work hard to find my niche.''

She lifted a spoonful of chocolate pudding, the stuff

Tucker called "mousse." "Something tells me that you aren't going to have any trouble."

It hit her that Tucker would always be lucky. He was that kind. She didn't hold it against him. It was a quality she rather admired.

After lunch he had put his arm over her shoulders and walked her back to the natural history museum. From the front doors of the museum, she watched him walk back across the Mall, the wind ruffling his blond hair. His shoulders were hunched against the wind and his hands were thrust in his pockets, but he walked lightly, almost jauntily.

She decided that it had been nice to have his arm around her. It was very possible, she thought, that she had at last hit upon someone to fall in love with.

THREE

Blake Farraby's indelible childhood memories of ski trips always featured staring down some awe-inspiring ravine while his father thundered, "Stop blubbering. We're here to ski, damn it, not to have fun!" Then there were the inevitable crashes. When Blake couldn't have been more than four or five he was being disentangled from innumerable pileups near trees or pulled out of snowdrifts, his teeth chattering.

Blake's father always picked the most uncomfortable places to go skiing. Dr. Farraby took his skiing fast and rough as a matter of principle. He intensely disliked trendy resorts where the people he called "Eurotrash" and "snow dumb bunnies" sat around fires drinking hot buttered rum.

The ski lodge he had chosen for the family's current excursion was precisely to his liking. Reveille at the huts was at dawn and after a scanty breakfast, the guests, demon skiers all, climbed into helicopters to be taken to inaccessible runs.

The incredible thrashing noise and the sight of the soft snow being whipped up by the fierce wind of the whirling rotors was frightening to Blake and he only just managed to keep from showing it. His mother squeezed her eyes shut as they took off but she didn't complain. If she disliked these Spartan outings, she never showed it. When Dr. Farraby decided on any course of action, he wouldn't tolerate disobedience from his family. "I can stand all the rest," Mrs. Farraby had confided once to Blake, "but I just hate it that they don't have bathrooms. I don't think it's too much to ask to have a bathroom when you're on vacation."

The copter deposited them at the top of the slope. Then it moved with a monotonous chopping sound downhill toward the pickup point. Blake gazed down an almost vertical slope adorned with patches of trees. "Look at that!" his father cried. "Never skied on. Beautiful!"

Mrs. Farraby uneasily fingered the radio transceiver that hung around her neck like a medallion. In those wilds everyone had to wear one in case of avalanche or accident.

"Okay," said Dr. Farraby. "Here we go! Follow me."

The cold air hit Blake's teeth with a shock as he pushed off, but he could already feel his blood heating with exhilaration. His father's relentless training had paid off. Although Blake didn't consider himself particularly brave, he found that when he was at the top of a mountain looking down, he was willing to try absolutely anything. The ski run didn't exist that intimidated him. He scarcely even noticed the transceiver bumping hard against his sternum, and he heard nothing but the wind whistling past his ears as he plummeted down the mountainside like a knife cutting through wind and snow.

He followed his father around a stand of trees, and when he skied a parallel curve, snow kicked into his teeth, he laughed softly to himself. It was amazing. As long as he was skiing down a mountain he had it all—speed, nerve, even grace. It was one of the few times in his life that he felt free. He wished it could go on forever, an endless slope of perfect powder.

Near the bottom of the slope, Mrs. Farraby managed to upend in a drift. Blake, his dad, and a couple of the other men had to trudge up after her and pull her out. Blake's dad massaged her feet. "This is so embarrassing," she murmured as they helped her up. Her teeth were chattering. Blake knew how she felt. He had done his time in snowdrifts. His mother's problem was that she hadn't begun when she was four, the way he had.

As they were tromping through the snow to the copter, Dr. Farraby muttered, "Your mother's a tough one, Blake. Just remember when you're doing the picking that a whining woman is the biggest pain in the world."

Blake was astonished to receive this advice. He couldn't remember that his father had ever said anything about women to him before. Did this mark some kind of recognition that he was growing up?

The skiers climbed back into the helicopter to be lifted to the top again. As Blake squeezed in the seat next to his mother, he tried to blot out memories of the movies he had seen where the copter went down in flames. He concentrated on regular breathing and on making his mind blank. Suddenly Rainey's face swam before his eyes. She must be tromping all around the Museum of Natural History about now. Although he hadn't let on, the trip to the museum had sounded deadly dull.

His father shouted over the noise of the copter. "This

spring we've got to take you around to see some colleges, son. It's time you started thinking about that.''

Sometimes Blake felt as if he were on some sort of ascending staircase—algebra, calculus, SATs, competitive college, life of achievement. He squeezed his eyes closed. ''I hate these blinking copters,'' he said.

''What did you say?'' his father yelled in his ear.

''Nothing!'' shouted Blake.

''I'm glad we didn't come when they had those Christmas crowds,'' his father yelled. ''This is really great skiing,''

Mrs. Farraby smiled wanly.

Ann Lee's mother had wanted to drive her to the interview in Raleigh, but Ann Lee thought that it would make her look too dependent on her mother. She had gotten a ride over with Susan instead. Now, as she waited in the hall for Susan to finish her interview, she regretted that decision.

At last the door opened and Ann Lee caught a glimpse of the smiling pink face of one of the interviewers. Susan came out and the door closed behind her.

''How did it go?'' Ann Lee inquired anxiously.

Susan reached for her coat and drew on her gloves. ''All right, I guess.''

''What did they ask you?''

''Oh, the usual stuff—tell us about yourself, what are your interests, that kind of thing. Then they said, tell us what you would do in the next ten minutes if you could do anything you wanted.''

''They asked me that, too. What did you say?''

''Lose ten pounds, ensure world peace, save the whales, teach my parakeet to say 'Go, West Mount,' and find a cure for acne and the common cold. What did you say?''

''I couldn't think of anything,'' Ann Lee said miserably.

"They don't expect you to give perfect answers. I think the big thing is to be yourself."

Ann Lee thought about the French Foreign Legion. That was one foolproof way to get out of town, but she wasn't sure they took women and it didn't seem at all likely that her parents would let her join up.

Susan shrugged herself into her coat. "Jesse and I are going out for pizza and a movie tonight. The reason I mention it is, just remember to act like you went when you're around my mom and dad, okay? They think I'm going with you."

Of all the boys at West Mount High that Susan could have fallen for, it seemed perverse of her to choose Jesse McCracken. Not that there was anything wrong with Jesse himself. But his family had been feuding with Susan's family ever since a bizarre incident the preceding spring. The Brantleys' big white dog, Muffin, had attacked the McCrackens' dog, Blue, in the parking lot of a fast-food restaurant and had nearly killed him. Jesse's dad, desperate to save Blue, had reached in his pickup for his rifle and shot Muffin. Hearing gunfire, Susan's dad ran outside. Just then Ben McCracken dumped Muffin's limp body off the bed of his pickup at the feet of the horrified Mr. Brantley.

Since then, Susan's dad couldn't hear the name McCracken without turning red. His eyes bulged at the thought of what had happened and anybody who got him on the subject of "trigger-happy rednecks" got a ten-minute blast of anger. Using his position as city councilman and chairman of the zoning committee, he had done what he could do to get back at the McCrackens—he fixed it so that a tacky trailer park was built across from their farmhouse. But even that didn't seem to make him feel materially better and Susan didn't dare mention Jesse's name at home.

Ann Lee felt suddenly tired of Susan and her complicated romance. It seemed too much to bear on top of all those clever comebacks to the interviewing committee. "How can your mom and dad think you're going out with me on a Saturday night? It doesn't make sense."

"I know. It's not too convincing, is it? I've got to come up with something better. But this will do for a while. Right now they just figure I'm between boys."

"But it's never going to work in the long run."

"Don't worry. In the long run I'll be going away to college and I can do what I want. In the short run, I have to live with my dad. Just help me with this. You know I'd do it for you."

Ann Lee felt too limp to argue. She pulled a knit cap down over her ears. "Okay."

"What did you say?"

"I said okay!"

"You don't have to yell at me!"

Ann Lee thought dismally that *okay* would be a suitable epitaph for her tombstone. No matter how hard she worked, no matter how often she tried, she never seemed to reach a higher plane than *okay*.

Sunday on the bus ride home most of the kids were asleep, worn out by the late hours they had kept the night before. While sophomores with flushed faces snoozed around her, Rainey thought about Tucker. She felt she had a decided advantage when it came to getting something going with him. He was transferring in at the middle of the term and it seemed reasonable to think he would be glad to see a friendly face. He certainly seemed glad to see her when he had spotted her at the museum. Remembering the way he had put his arm around her, she closed her eyes and smiled. The details of how her romance would unfold were not, of course, perfectly plain at the moment, but on the whole she felt optimistic.

It had always seemed to her that boys were easier to manage than girls. Susan and Ann Lee, for instance, were always pleasant enough, but their words skated along a surface she couldn't pierce. She suspected them of spending hours over at each other's houses fussing with each other's hair and hashing over people's hidden motives. She sometimes had the feeling when they were talking that she was missing the nuances. It was as if they were speaking in French. In contrast, boys like Blake and Michael were straightforward. They didn't say as much, but what they did say had no hidden meanings. In her opinion boys were simple creatures. There was no reason why Tucker should be an exception.

At last all the students and chaperons were dropped off at the West Mount High parking lot, where lights shone on a collection of station wagons and sedans in which parents sat waiting. Rainey's ancient vehicle stood out among them, a vehicle of unsurpassed age and ugliness. In her eyes its very ugliness conferred distinction on it. This was no nondescript suburban station wagon. It had history and character. Equally important, it belonged to her and it ran.

Her legs felt stiff when she got off the bus, and she tottered a bit as she walked to her car. Getting in it, she sniffed the familiar, faintly doggy aroma of the interior as she threw her carryall in the backseat. It felt good to be back.

A few minutes later she drove up to the blinking red and purple sign that said "Starlight Trailer Park." She saw at once a light glowing through the curtains of her living room. That was puzzling. Her mom shouldn't be home yet. The weekend was the busy time at the Carolina Bar and Grill and she wasn't supposed to get off till eleven. Had she gotten sick? Rainey jumped out of the car and charged in the front door. "Mom?"

Her breath sucked in suddenly when she glimpsed a man's figure silhouetted in her bedroom. She reached into the tiny kitchen and grabbed a knife. Then, keeping her eyes on the bedroom, she began to back out of the trailer.

A low laugh surprised her. "Rainey, hon, what kind of a welcome is that for Pappa?"

Her pulse was pounding in her ears and her vision became blurred. "Pappa?"

Her father leaned in the bedroom doorway, fingering his beard. "You don't like the beard, huh?"

She took a ragged breath. "Jeez, you scared me. In fact, you just about scared me to death."

"Sorry about that. I didn't think that I'd scare you," he said apologetically. "When I got here, I just walked in."

"How did you get here?" Rainey asked.

"I walked."

"You walked—from where?" She felt a little dizzy.

"From the bus station. It was a little dicey coming through town, but I had a hat on, pulled way down, and I limped to disguise the way I move. Lots of times you can tell a person more by how he moves than by his face. Then when I got past downtown I walked along the power lines. The power company clears a path for them right through the woods. It's easy walking."

"You can't stay here. Mom—"

He raised a hand. "I wouldn't think of bothering your mom. In fact, it might be better if you don't even mention my visit to her."

"I guess Aunt Sadie told you about the divorce."

"She did mention it. It made me think I'd better not count on a welcome from Rose." He sat down on the couch and began leafing through the television guide. "Anything good on?"

"But you can't stay here!"

"Didn't I just tell you I wasn't going to bother your mom? I'm going to bed down in that old tobacco barn I saw out past the woods across the road. It's just that I know there's not going to be much to do once I get there, so I thought I'd watch a little television before I go."

Rainey collapsed into the armchair breathing heavily. "Where have you been? All this time—"

"All over. It's a big country. I worked as a dishwasher in New York until the restaurant closed down. So then I got a lead on a job in South Carolina, but it didn't pan out. I'm kind of limited. I got a social security number under a phony name, but I've had to steer clear of driving. Do you notice how they're always raking people like me in on traffic violations? I figured out early on it would be better to get rid of my car, but the trouble is there aren't too many jobs you can get with no car and no questions asked."

"You need money," she said in a hollow voice.

He looked pleased. "You always were smart, Rainey. I like the way you just jumped ahead to that. Very sharp. The thing is, if I can just get back to New York I've got connections up there. If worse comes to worst I can bolt to the reservation there. The cops haven't come on the reservation yet. It's not even sure they've got a legal right to do it. Anyway, they've never tried. So it's good to fall back on. Makes you feel kind of secure. But I've got to have the bus fare to New York, first, plus some money to keep me until I make my connections."

"How much do you need?"

"Well, the bus fare's sixty-four bucks, plus enough to keep me for a while—I figure about two hundred minimum."

"That much?" She licked her lips. "I just spent every penny I had on this field trip. I won't get paid for a week and even then it's not much. What about Aunt Sadie? Couldn't she help you out?"

"What do you think? I went there first. I'm really up against it or I wouldn't be coming here bothering you, hon."

"You're not bothering me. But I just don't see how we're going to manage."

He fished a handful of change out of his pocket and spread it out on his palm. "One dollar and sixty-seven cents." He shook his head. "If it was spring I could sign on with some migrant crew until I got a little stake, but there just isn't much going this time of year. You don't know anybody who needs a dishwasher real cheap, do you?"

"You can't work around here! You can't go out in public. Somebody would be bound to see you. It's not like up in New York where you don't know anybody."

"It's a problem all right. You know, I think I'd better help myself to some provisions from your mom's kitchen. It looks like I may have to hang around a bit."

Rainey got up and went into the kitchen. Since the kitchen was an alcove off the living room, they could continue talking uninterrupted. There was something unreal about having her father sitting in the living room. She realized that her mental image of him had not been perfectly distinct. Seeing him now, he seemed oddly familiar and at the same time strange. It was hard to take in the fact of his presence.

She pulled a large paper bag out of the closet and a package of plastic sandwich bags out from under the sink. If she didn't want her mother to notice the missing food, she'd have to take just a little bit of each thing. She tossed in a couple of apples, a hunk of cheese, a few pieces of bread, a handful of cookies, whatever could be eaten without cooking.

"I can't get over how you've grown, Rainey. Your aunt told me, but I hadn't imagined it. You're a regular young lady now. And one heck of a pretty one, too. It's real good to see you. Tell me what you're up to these days."

Rainey threw in some napkins and a plastic cup. "There's not much to tell. I'm a junior. I'm starting to think about college. The money is going to be a problem, though."

"Don't forget you're on the tribal roll. You're my kid just as much as you're your mother's and you might be able to get a scholarship because you're an Indian."

"We'll see." She threw in a few packages of chocolate and peanut butter cups. Her mother would think she had gone on a wild eating jag, but her father was a big man, and she couldn't expect him to get by with a few celery sticks. She rolled the top of the bag over. "I'm going to have to bring you some more later. If I take a whole bunch of food all at once she's going to notice."

"What do you think, Rainey? Would Rose turn me in?"

Rainey hesitated. "Maybe you'd better not risk it."

He sighed. "I guess you're right. It's too bad. It would sure be a lot easier if we could tell her."

"Just give me some time. I'll come up with something, but I've got to have time to think."

"It is great to be home again. I don't really like it all that much up north." He leaned back on the couch and picked up the remote control. "Hey!" he cried. " 'Murder, She Wrote.' Aw-right!"

Rainey couldn't believe he was going to sit on the couch and watch television. But what else was there for him to do, really?

Every dog in the trailer park was sure to start barking when he left. She'd have to provide some cover. Maybe she would take out the garbage and rattle the cans.

"You can't cut right across the road to go back to that tobacco barn," she warned him. "Jesse McCracken and his family live in that farmhouse, and they've got five or six hounds that run loose all the time."

"I noticed that. Maybe you'd better drive me down the road a ways. Then I can loop back through the woods. That should be okay."

She couldn't understand how he could be so calm. But, then, a jumpy man could never have done the things he'd done. She remembered how it had come out that the day he had taken the hostages, he had walked into a feed store and bought a shotgun and a saw. Within the hour he had sawed off the shotgun, taken three hostages, and was phoning in statements to the newspaper. He had gone one step at a time, all very simple and straightforward. It was a method that had seemed to work okay as far as it went.

"I don't want you to put off leaving because if you wait too late Mom might come in."

"Don't worry. I'll go as soon as the show is over."

"It might look funny if I go driving off late at night, too."

He nodded absently. She supposed he was already engrossed in the show. She only wished she were. She went into her room and got her flashlight to put in the bag. After a minute's thought, she added a package of matches and a few vitamin pills. She noticed a heavy quilted jacket lying on the couch, but still he was going to need something to sleep on. She got an old blanket from her bedroom closet and stuck it into a plastic dry-cleaning bag. If the ground was damp, he could put the dry cleaning bag down under the blanket.

An hour later, when it was time for her father to go, Rainey carried out the kitchen garbage bag and rattled the tops of the cans as she had planned. The trailer park dogs yipped frantically. After a moment she heard the gruffer protests of the McCracken's hounds across the road. She had been careful to turn off the porch light so her father wouldn't be seen when he went out of the front door. When she went around front to her car he was already sitting in the passenger seat.

"Where'd you get the car?" he asked.

"I bought it." She put the key in the ignition. "I got a very good price on it."

"It sure is nice to have a car and not have to fiddle with bus schedules and all that junk."

"Yup."

"You're not mad at me for coming around, are you, Rainey?"

"Why would I be mad at you?"

"I just don't want to be a burden to you, that's all."

"It's okay. Don't worry about it."

Rainey drove a quarter of a mile down the road and let him off by the woods just past the McCracken's farm. When she got back to the trailer, she realized that her stomach felt light and queasy. It was shock, she supposed.

Her head was whirling in a confusion of ideas and feelings. Her father had dropped out of her life in the midst of blazing publicity. Now he had dropped silently back into it, but no one knew. She wasn't sure how she felt about it yet. She remembered one day when there hadn't been enough cash on hand for lunch money and she had watched her mother stomp around the kitchen making mayonnaise and bread sandwiches. "So we're all going to be heroes, huh? I guess I'll just quit my job and go out west and campaign for the rights of grape pickers, right? Just let my kid starve to death while I worry about the grape pickers and everybody else in the world. That's right. Charity begins at home, that's what I say.''

Rainey never had been able to work out the right and wrong of what her father had done. It was too confusing. Particularly when she was so personally involved. Somebody had to worry about making the world a better place, as her father had said. And going through channels never got you anywhere since the establishment had all the power and for practical purposes ordinary people had none. But taking hostages didn't seem like the nicest way to go about demanding change. After all, the hostages couldn't be expected to know that her father didn't intend to hurt them. They were probably permanent nervous wrecks. And as it turned out what he had done hadn't accomplished much either. Except that it had messed up a lot of people's lives.

Or was that fair? It wasn't as if he had tried on purpose to mess up her life or her mother's.

Only one thing was certain. Her father was camped in that stinking tobacco barn behind the McCracken's place and it looked as if he was going to stay there until she came up with the money to send him on his way.

Rainey jumped when the front door opened. Her mother stepped heavily into the room. "What are you doing sitting here practically in the dark?" Mrs. Locklear switched on the light by the couch. "You aren't sick, are you?"

"I've just got a headache."

"You better take an aspirin. Well, how was the trip?" The couch squeaked as Mrs. Locklear fell onto it. The flesh of her round face sagged a little under the eyes and her dark hair was shot through with gray. It seemed to Rainey that her mother looked older than her father and more tired. Maybe, she thought, it was from worrying. Her father probably saved a lot of energy by not worrying. She only wished she had inherited the knack.

Mrs. Locklear lifted her skirt and sniffed at the hem. "Do you smell something? I swear, it smells like tobacco. There's enough smoke at work, but it doesn't seem like it's on my clothes."

"I don't smell anything," said Rainey quickly.

"I guess it must be my imagination. So, tell me about the trip, sugar. How did it go?"

Rainey cast her mind back over the trip. It seemed weeks before. "Well, I ran into this boy I used to go to school with. He's coming back to West Mount. So that was interesting."

"Is he a nice boy?"

"Uh-huh."

Later on, as Rainey lay in bed, she remembered the broken pane in the back where her father had reached in to unlatch the door. She was going to have to get that pane fixed somehow. It was some time before she fell into a fitful sleep.

FOUR

_T_he next day Rainey decided it wouldn't be safe to hire somebody to fix the broken pane, even if she could have found someone who would do it cheaply. She went by the glass store and bought a sheet of window glass and a glass cutter on her way to work. That evening she scored the glass with the cutter and tapped the pane along the line as the man at the glass store had instructed her to do. She had never cut glass before and when she tapped it, it didn't break quite cleanly. Also she had to use a lot of putty to get the pane stuck in the door. Once she had finished, she could see that it didn't quite match the other panes. The putty around it was too new and looked thick and messy, but she didn't think her mother would notice. She turned off the outside lights, then went out back and put the leftover glass and putty into the garbage can where no one would find it.

After her mother came in, Rainey's eyes kept creeping nervously to the replaced pane. It took a strong effort of will to keep herself from looking fixedly at the back door and she was glad when it was time to go to bed.

Hours later she woke up with a horrible thought—water. She hadn't given her father anything to drink!

She felt clammy all over. It was hopeless for her to try to get back to sleep, and as soon as the sky began to lighten outside she got up. She could hear her mother snoring gently as she began to fill an empty gallon milk jug with water. The sound of the water running in the pipes seemed incredibly loud, and she held her breath, afraid her mother might wake. Next she packed up some more provisions and sneaked out the trailer. She drove by way of a back road to the pasture where the tobacco barn lay. She was bracing herself to find her father's dried-out body. Something seemed to be stuck in her throat and her heart was fluttering. How long could a person go without water? But when she parked her car among some trees and got out, she spotted a cement water trough in the pasture and went limp with relief. He had enough water, after all.

She got a grip on the bag of provisions and the container of water and clambered awkwardly over the rusty barbed wire fence. It was almost light now and she could see pretty well, but the air had the cold, dead feel of early morning. The McCrackens' hounds began to howl. She shivered and reminded herself that they were trained to stay in the yard.

Some half-grown calves trotted over to her eagerly, under the delusion she was bringing them bottles of milk. "Shoo," she said. "Go away." She was finding it difficult to move through the pasture even without the problem of the curious calves. The pasture had been roughly cut, and clumps and tufts of the dry grass kept tripping her up. The calves bumped

36

against her with their heads. She could feel their hot breath on her neck. There was a crackling sound as one nibbled experimentally at the bag of provisions. Holding the paper bag up over her head, she stumbled forward. She sneaked a quick glance at the ground. She was hoping to avoid stepping in anything. "Go away!" she told the calves. At last she reached the other side of the field. With a final ineffectual "Shoo!" at the calves, she separated the fence wires and crawled through.

The tobacco barn was old and dilapidated. Its green roof sagged as if it were melting into the earth, and the gaping hole that served as a door revealed a black and pungent interior. Her father appeared suddenly and spat on the dirt. "It's faster to go by the way of the woods."

"But it's not safer." Safer was something he was not terrifically concerned with, Rainey supposed, or he would not have chosen a career as a fugitive. She put the gallon jug of water down on the dirt and gave him the paper bag. "It's all there. Peanut butter, jelly, bread, Mars bars. Don't forget to take your vitamin pills."

"Don't think I'm not grateful, Rainey. This stuff is great. But have you got any line on how we can get ahold of some money? This place ain't exactly the Hilton." He glanced behind him at the dark interior of the barn, which smelled strongly of damp and tobacco.

"I get paid Saturday, but with what I can manage to save from that it'll be at least a month before I get two hundred dollars. I've got to think of something else."

"Doesn't Rose have any money laid by for emergencies? You might be able to skim a little off that without her noticing it."

"No," Rainey said shortly. "She doesn't. Just hang on. I'll figure something out."

"Sure you will, honeybunch. I'm not worried."

Rainey had often thought that a little more money might be convenient, but she had never before felt as desperate for money as she did now.

She was able to slip back into the trailer without anyone seeing her. There were no signs of life in the trailer park yet, and her mother was still snoring softly. She ate a bowl of cereal, changed her clothes, fixed herself a sandwich and drove to school. It was up to her to take care of her father and to get together the money he needed. What's more, she had to do it before someone saw him. The responsibility seemed overwhelming. She felt as if lead weights were attached to her hands and feet.

When she got to school, everything looked strange and distant, as if she were looking through the wrong end of binoculars.

Kids were milling around talking outside the buildings as usual. Bleakly, she wondered what they could possibly be talking about that was of any interest. Clothes, basketball, English tests—all seemed trivial to her compared to the question of what to do about her father. She went through homeroom in a daze.

"Yo, Rainey!" Blake was leaning on the door to creative writing class. He beamed at her as if he didn't have a trouble in the world. Very possibly, she realized, with surprise, he didn't.

"Hey, Blake, how was the"—she racked her brain—"uh, skiing?" she finished triumphantly.

"Fantastic. What about the museum?"

"Nice."

"We just got back—late last night. Did I miss anything important?"

She hesitated, then shook her head. Of course, her own life had been turned inside out since Blake had set off for a few days of skiing, but she couldn't tell him that.

Rainey followed Blake into the classroom feeling rather as if an alien were inhabiting her body. The person inside her who was fiercely trying to lay her hand on two hundred dollars seemed to have no relationship at all to the person who took a seat in the classroom.

While Mrs. Armstrong called roll, Rainey noticed that Tucker had arrived. He was sitting in the front row in tight faded jeans, a baggy T-shirt, and a tweed jacket. He winked at her and her heart began to thump so hard she thought her face might be giving her away.

Susan handed Rainey a note for Ann Lee. Under the fold, Rainey glimpsed the word *Tucker!!!!!*****. In the past Rainey had thought Susan's habit of overstatement silly, but today it seemed to strike the right note.

Rainey was almost desperately glad to see Tucker. The heated air in the classroom felt suffocatingly close. Even the gray skies outside the windows seemed to be closing in on her. She knew the problem was her father. Knowing that he was hiding in the tobacco barn polluted everything. But Tucker was apart from all that. He was squeaky clean, light-hearted, and vaguely irresponsible. She simply couldn't imagine him desperate for money.

"Get that," Michael muttered in her ear. "Tucker's back in town. You figure that prep school got too hot for him or what?"

"Maybe he just got tired of it," Rainey whispered.

"Class, we have a new student with us today," Mrs. Armstrong announced. "Tucker Harrison."

"Harbisson," corrected Tucker.

"Sorry. Tucker Harbisson. He's from around here, though. He's been going to Saint Anselm's, so I expect some of you already know him. Tucker tells me that his primary interest is fiction. It looks as if we have another short-story writer in our midst. I think we're just going to have a super edition of *Endnotes* this year.'' During the first semester, Mrs. Armstrong had taken a class at East Carolina University on teaching creative writing and ever since she had been fired up with enthusiasm. Right at the moment Rainey was finding all the enthusiasm hard to take.

Mrs. Armstrong rested her fingertips on her desk and leaned toward the class eagerly. ''People, I told you to be thinking about a sustained effort now, a coherent work of art, perhaps a short story for our spring publication. We're going to devote this class period to letting you begin your rough drafts, if you haven't already done so.''

Rainey had forgotten all about the story they needed to write for the class's spring publication. Mrs. Armstrong had been burbling on about it for a week. They were to have a bake sale to supplement the money they got from the student activity fee so their magazine would look slick and professional. They were supposed to polish each well-chosen noun, verb, and adjective to dazzling perfection.

Tucker smiled in Rainey's direction. Suddenly self-conscious, she looked away.

''Remember, class, at this stage, you want to stay loose. Creativity is messy. Your ideas will simply boil up from your unconscious now and we'll worry about the sentence structure later. I want you to start writing and keep writing. Begin—now!''

Rainey poised her purple pen over her notebook paper. After she scribbled her name, her pen began to move swiftly over the paper.

The green slime oozed up the back steps of the trailer. It slurped and sloshed against the back door, groping, sucking until its formless tentacles touched an edge of broken glass. Its dim mind did not take in that a pane of the back door had been broken. It only knew it had found the opening it was looking for. It sniffled, making a disgusting sound like the last bit of soapy water going down the bathtub drain. It had smelled human flesh!

Mrs. Armstrong was walking through the classroom peering over people's shoulders, making sure no one was writing a letter. She paused by Rainey's desk for some time. Rainey's hand moved slower and slower. Finally she looked up.

"Don't let me stop you!" Mrs. Armstrong blinked and moved on to the next desk.

Rainey stared at her paper, a bitter taste in her mouth. She remembered now that the story she had originally planned to write had been about a golden-haired princess in a tower. That was before her life had been taken over by the anxiety that seeped into every corner of her mind. Now it seemed to her as if she weren't just writing a horror story— she was living one.

When she had written a few pages of her rough draft, she began chewing on her pen. She jotted some numbers at the corner of the sheet. At three dollars and fifty cents, twenty hours a week equaled seventy dollars, minus gas and oil equaled, say, fifty-five dollars. Suppose she drove absolutely no place but work and school. She wondered how much she would save that way. She scribbled over the figures as the bell rang. It seemed hopeless.

Rainey had planned to accidentally bump into Tucker after class, but Mrs. Armstrong stopped her as she was making for the door.

"Can I talk to you, Rainey?"

"Yes, ma'am." Rainey's knees suddenly felt wobbly. She realized that what she needed most right then was to be inconspicuous. She needed to remain unnoticed until she got her father out of town.

Mrs. Armstrong looked at her anxiously. "I know I asked you to let your unconscious boil up, but I have to admit I was a little surprised at your rough draft. It was so different from the sort of work you've done in the past."

"I've gotten interested in the fantasy, horror, and science-fiction genres."

"Of course, some good work has been done in those fields, and I don't want to restrict you in any way. I want those creative juices to just *flow*. So I hope you aren't going to take this the wrong way." Mrs. Armstrong's brows were tightly squeezed into an expression of concern. "But is anything bothering you that you need to talk about?"

Rainey made her face a blank. "No, everything's fine."

Mrs. Armstrong looked at her doubtfully. "Just keep in mind that if you need somebody to talk to, I'm here for you."

"I better go. I'm going to be late."

By the time Rainey got out to the hall it was almost empty. Everyone had gone on to the next class, including Tucker. It figured.

At lunchtime, Rainey got her brown lunch bag from her locker. She waited in the hall until she thought people had had time to get their trays, then she went on into the cafeteria. To her surprise, Michael was sitting with Blake. She dropped her brown bag on their table and sat down. "I thought you were having lunch with Cynthia these days, Michael."

"Yeah, well, she's gone for a job interview. And listen, Blake, don't you mention a word about this to anybody. It's strictly hush-hush."

"I don't exactly spend a lot of time hanging out at the hospital, you know."

"Yeah, but with your dad being over there and everything it could get around."

"Pull yourself together, man. I'm not interested. I'm not going to squeal on Cynthia."

"Of course, I hope the interview goes okay, but then again I don't, if you follow me."

"Did somebody say interview?" Ann Lee was gripping her tray so tightly her knuckles were white.

"We're not talking about you, Ann Lee." Rainey pulled her sandwich out of its bag. "Honestly, we're not."

"I ought to hear from the committee some time next month." Ann Lee sat down abruptly.

Rainey spotted Tucker coming out of the lunch line. When she waved he veered sharply in their direction.

"I didn't know you knew Tucker." Blake frowned at her.

"We ran into each other at the museum."

Tucker plopped his tray down on the table and sprawled in a chair. "It is so great to be back." A grin widened on his face. "All the noise in the halls, the commotion, the indifference—"

"The girls," interrupted Michael.

"Yeah, that, too. Man, I love it here."

"Don't you think you'll miss the individual attention you got at prep school?" Ann Lee asked. "I expect the math and the science here aren't quite as good, either. We don't get as much lab time as we should."

Tucker didn't seem to hear her. He was looking all around the cafeteria. "It's like a candy store. There's so much going on."

"So what'd you get kicked out for Tucker?" Michael regarded him with detachment. "Booze, girls, cheating?"

43

"Michael's always teasing." Rainey looked at Michael uneasily.

"Oh, I know Michael." Tucker smiled. "He doesn't bother me. No, I just got tired of Saint Anselm's. I had the feeling I was missing out on a lot of fun at home, and I'm beginning to see I was right."

Michael shook Tucker's hand. "And we're just as glad to have you back among us, Tucker old bean. You'd better believe it."

Tucker laughed. "Still crazy after all these years, huh, Michael?"

Blake turned to Rainey. "Since when did you start bringing your lunch?"

She started guiltily. "Just today. I just started today." She figured she had to save every penny she could. Packing her own lunch wouldn't help that much but every little bit counted.

"You're the smart one," Blake said. "I mean, when they put something on the menu board and actually call it 'mystery meat,' you know you're in trouble."

Overwhelmingly conscious of her real motives, Rainey felt her hands grow cold. She didn't have much to add to the conversation at the table from then on. She was preoccupied with adding up figures in her head, trying to figure out when she could come up with two hundred dollars. It was a futile exercise but she had become obsessed by it. No matter how many times she added it up, the money never seemed to mount up fast enough. Her father couldn't stay in that tobacco barn for a whole month. For one thing, as the weather warmed up and people started spending more time outside, it would get more and more risky. It was bad enough already with Mr. McCracken going back to the pasture twice a day to feed the calves. Suppose he came unexpectedly some time and her father didn't have time to take cover.

At a nearby table, Susan was watching. "Look. There's Tucker. Moving in on Rainey. He didn't waste any time."

"Where's he been? I thought maybe he moved away or something," said Jesse.

"No, he just went to prep school. As far as I know his dad's business is doing okay, so it can't be that they're economizing. I guess he must not have liked it there or maybe he got kicked out."

Jesse raised an eyebrow. "You don't like him or what?"

"Oh, I like him okay. He's actually kind of fun."

Jesse smiled. "Just don't like him too much."

"As if you had anything to worry about."

"Look, if you'd rather be over there where the action is, it looks like they could fit in two more."

Susan hesitated. "Do you want to move over there? If you want to, it's okay with me."

"Don't ask me. They're your friends, not mine."

"It's just that we don't get to see that much of each other as it is." She lifted Jesse's fingers off the table, one by one, and looked into his eyes. "I like it here, just the two of us."

The truth was that Susan did feel a pang of regret about leaving her old lunch table. The social game was one she had played exceedingly well and now that she and Jesse ate over in a corner together, sometimes she felt out of it, almost isolated. When she found herself feeling that way, though, she was quick to reproach herself for being shallow. She loved Jesse and he loved her. That was all that mattered.

She watched his face, trying to read his thoughts. He was staring fixedly down at his hamburger in a way that made her almost nervous.

"I tell you what," he said, "tonight, why don't we get something to eat before we go to the mall."

"We can eat at the mall. There are all those places right by the theater. I mean, true, the food's not that *good*, but—"

"It's just there's no privacy, Susan. Everybody's at the mall on Friday night. It's like the fireworks on the Fourth of July."

"I know what! I'll meet you at the mall early and we can go someplace from there. Anyplace you want."

"Okay," he said shortly.

"Did I say something wrong?"

He shook his head. "Tell me the truth. Doesn't it get you down, sneaking around like this?"

"I don't exactly like it, if that's what you mean. But I'd like it a lot less if my dad started screaming at me. Do your parents know you're out with me?" She shot him a challenging look.

"Okay. I haven't exactly mentioned it, but it's not like I'm lying or anything. I don't have to sneak around. I just *go*."

"It's different with boys. I wish I were a boy, then I could go anyplace I wanted and come in any old time and nobody would say a thing."

"I don't."

"Huh?"

"Wish you were a boy."

She grinned. "Stupid. Is it all set then? I'll meet you in front of the theaters at, say, six, and then we'll go off someplace."

"Someplace dark."

"But someplace where we can get food."

"Picky, picky."

Susan loved the honey color of Jesse's skin and the sun-washed look of his straight, fair hair. Sometimes when she remembered that this decent, good-looking guy was in love with her, she could hardly believe it and she found herself gazing at him with wonder.

He was checking out Rainey's table again. "You know, I saw something this morning—it was kind of weird. Rainey was out in our east pasture. I mean, we're talking first thing this morning, before breakfast even. I only went out back to make the dogs shut up. It looked to me like she was carrying something."

"She was over at your place? What could she be doing there?"

Jesse didn't feel it was tactful to point out that Rainey had lived right across the street ever since Susan's dad had got the trailer park built there. He squirted ketchup on his burger. "I don't know. It's not that I actually care. There's nothing in that back pasture but some calves and that old tobacco barn. We put the calves back there on purpose because a long time ago we had some trouble with the tobacco barn. A motorcycle gang was hanging out there and using it for a drug hideout. But now we go out there in a regular way to feed the calves and keep an eye on things."

Susan shivered. "A motorcycle gang. Yuck."

"Oh, it was bad. The police were out there and arrested a bunch of them. After that we cleared some trees between that pasture and the house. Now it's not so cut off."

Susan leaned toward him. "You don't think Rainey's mixed up in drugs! Is that what you're hinting at?"

"Nah! That other stuff was all years and years ago. I was just a kid when it happened. It just made me think—well, it's just funny, that's all."

"Maybe she was just working on some science project or something. Remember in ninth grade when we had to make

47

that insect collection? I ended up poking around in the weirdest places—fields, storm sewers, garbage dumps. Places I'd *never* go to if I hadn't been looking for bugs.''

"Yeah, I guess it could have been something like that." But when Jesse looked back at Rainey's table later, he was thoughtful.

That afternoon the skies cleared and the sunshine was like a bright premonition of spring. When Blake got home from school, he glanced up at the clear blue sky and decided to grab the chance to wash his car. He had not been able to bring himself to trust it to a car wash and every fleck of dust that lodged on it made him cringe. He brought a bucket of sudsy water out and began soaping it with almost religious concentration.

He loved his car. Mostly he was kept pretty busy getting his homework done, keeping his parents off his back, and trying to make sure he had good enough grades to get into a decent college. Not much time was left for the messier emotions. Anything that he felt along those lines was sublimated into his car. The Corvette represented Blake's taste for beauty, his passion for speed, his lust for power, his fantasy of endless willing girls, even his stifled anger. The Vette was to Blake as victory is to basketball teams. He was rinsing it with a soft spray of water, almost holding his breath, when Susan's voice startled him.

"Hi!"

He wheeled around. Susan was jogging in place and dressed in a navy sweatshirt and sweat pants that were baggy at the knees. In old clothes and with a kerchief tied around her frizzed hair, she scarcely looked like herself.

"Since when did you take up jogging?"

She fanned her face with her hand. "Just started," she

panted. She hadn't actually taken up jogging. Looking out her second-story bedroom window across her backyard she had seen that Blake was washing his car, and she had been so starved for gossip that she had thrown on her sister's jogging clothes and run full speed around the block in order to encounter him casually. "It's a great way to keep in shape," she added.

"You better not stop all of a sudden like that. You're supposed to keep at it, and slow down gradually."

"Oh? Like this?" Susan jogged a few steps in place. "Well, what's up?"

"Hang on, I don't want to let the soap dry on the finish."

Susan's next words were drowned out by the sound of water blasting full force against the car.

"I saw Tucker having lunch with you," Susan said, loudly.

"Yeah."

"Did he tell you why he left Saint Anselm's?" asked Susan.

"Hey, you've stopped jogging again. You know you've got to keep at it until you get to your target pulse rate or it doesn't do you any good."

"Would you cut that out!" She plopped down behind the car, sitting cross-legged on the damp grass. "I don't care about my target pulse rate, so would you shut up about it?"

"I thought you were trying to get in shape."

"Well, I'll get in shape some other time. Tell me about Tucker."

"I didn't know you were interested in Tucker." He stared at her.

"I am *not* interested in Tucker, idiot. Not the way you're talking about, anyway. Don't you have any simple curiosity? Don't you just kind of like to know what's going on?"

He began wiping his car dry. "I guess not."

After a second's thought, she sent out another trial balloon. "Well, I thought it was interesting that he went to sit at your lunch table. It's not like he was ever buddies with you or Michael."

"That's for sure."

"That's what I thought. I mean, he only lives a few blocks from here, but I've never seen you two together."

"So what are you getting at, Susan?"

"I think he's interested in Rainey!"

Blake was so startled he dropped his cloth. He looked at it regretfully. Now he couldn't even use it. There might be grains of sand on it or something. "That's the stupidest thing I ever heard."

"Or I guess it could be Ann Lee." Susan didn't really believe that, but as Ann Lee's friend she felt she could not in good conscience rule it out.

"Okay, I take it back. That other thing wasn't the stupidest thing—what you just said, is. He isn't interested in Ann Lee, Susan. Jeez, you know him better than that. Half the things he likes to do, Ann Lee's mommy won't let her."

Susan sat on her hands. "It must be Rainey then. He's not a snob, you know."

"I'll give you that much. He's not a snob."

"I mean, he wouldn't care about Rainey being poor and about her dad and all. And she is good-looking."

Blake stared at her. "You know, Susan. You need a hobby or something. This way you like to talk about people is pitiful."

"And you're above it all, huh? You're just not interested."

"Right. I'm not."

Susan was still feeling a little lightheaded from all the

unaccustomed exercise. True, Blake's response had not been encouraging and right now he was looking at her in a very odd way, but she didn't let that stop her. She was enjoying herself. "Jesse saw Rainey in their back pasture early this morning—very early. I think Jesse figures it has something to do with drugs. There's an old tobacco barn that was used as a place to stash drugs before. Or, of course," she added fairly, "it could be something to do with a school project. I told him that."

Blake squirted the hose full on his taillights and a shower of ricocheting water hit Susan full in the face.

"Blake!" she shrieked. She leapt up.

He regarded her with satisfaction. "Sorry."

She hugged herself, her teeth chattering. "Now I'm freezing to death."

"Gee, that's too bad. Maybe you'd better go home and dry off. I've got to go in and get myself another old T-shirt, anyway. This one got dropped in the dirt."

"Brr," said Susan. Shooting Blake a suspicious glance, she jogged back to the sidewalk.

"Faster," he yelled. "and you need to keep up a steady pace!" He went in his front door and closed it firmly behind him.

After Susan went around the block to her house, she took a hot shower and washed her hair. Wrapped in her thickest bathrobe, a towel wound round her head, she curled up on her bed and dialed Ann Lee's number.

"Ann Lee? Guess what! I think Blake is getting this thing for Rainey. No kidding! Okay, I'll tell you why I think so. . . ." Susan grinned into the telephone receiver. She was where she liked to be—right in the center of things.

I don't see why I have to go," Ann Lee said fretfully.

"You have to go because the Harbissons invited you, that's why. They probably want to have somebody of Tucker's own generation there." It was Friday night and Mrs. Smith was dressed in her beaded blue crepe. "They can hardly serve him a tray in his room," she went on, "and he's certainly not going to be interested in what a bunch of his parents' middle-aged friends have to say."

"Mom, Tucker doesn't want to talk to me. Believe me."

"Why, that is completely absurd. You are a charming young woman and you must stop this business of selling yourself short. You can talk to him about all the things that young people are interested in these days—school, colleges, that kind of thing." Her mother gestured vaguely.

"Do I have to?"

"Yes. But keep in mind that Tucker is not as serious minded as you. He's not going to want to discuss the national debt. And be sure to let him do most of the talking—draw him out. That's what young men like. It makes them feel important. Ask his opinion about things. Don't be too fast to parade your own opinions. And above all, keep it light." She smiled. "I'm sure you'll be perfectly fine."

Ann Lee, her confidence completely sapped by her mother's detailed instructions, was unable to return the smile.

Twenty minutes later she meekly followed her parents in through the Harbisson's front doorway. Mrs. Smith brushed a dry cheek against Mrs. Harbisson's face while Mr. Harbisson boomed at them. "What can I get you? The usual, or do you want to risk one of Thelma's banana daiquiries?"

Mrs. Harbisson took Mrs. Smith's coat from her and hung it in the foyer closet. "Tell me, Mary, have you heard anything yet from that foreign study program?"

"No, and I'm on pins and needles. You know how I feel about that. At this point, I'm really halfway hoping it doesn't come through. Ann Lee's never been away from home before, and if she picks up and goes to Europe or South America I'll be a nervous wreck the entire summer."

"Oh, she'll be fine," protested Mr. Smith.

"She's never even peeled an apple for herself!" cried Mrs. Smith. "What would she do all by herself in a strange country where they don't speak English?"

"But you did say they live with families," said Mrs. Harbisson.

"Oh, yes. We never would have agreed to it if it hadn't been for that. But what do we know about these people? What if they're awful? What if Ann Lee doesn't get along with them?"

Pretending not to hear them, Ann Lee examined the picture hanging in the foyer. It looked rather like an abstract depiction of Humpty Dumpty sitting on a wall. Could that be what it was?

"You know the Thurmans and the Maxwells, don't you? They're here tonight. And the Turners. They're new in town. He's the administrator of the hospital since Bill Levy left." Mrs. Harbisson smiled vaguely in Ann Lee's direction as she led them into the living room. "Tucker ought to be out in a minute. He's watching some stupid rock video. I don't suppose you have any trouble with those at your house, do you?"

"Oh, no," Mrs. Smith said promptly. "Ann Lee likes only classical music."

Ann Lee wished she could disappear as conveniently as Tucker had. She sat in a big armchair and scanned the photos the Harbissons had arranged in silver frames on a nearby chest—Tucker sailing over a fence on a horse; Tucker in a dinner jacket accompanied by a pretty girl; Tucker's older sister, Allison, in a white evening gown accompanied by an ugly boy; all the Harbissons squinting into the sun in front of some Greek ruin.

Tucker and Ann Lee had been in the same class once or twice in grade school yet it would probably be possible to actually count the words he had addressed to her. Now she was going to have to spend an evening with him ignoring her. It was such a mistake to have come. At times like this she yearned to escape her parents with a passion that would have amazed them.

The adults had launched into a discussion of the short-comings of public education. "But what can you do?" Mrs. Harbisson exclaimed. "Both Allison and Tucker *wanted* to go to public school. Of course, neither of them is a scholar like Ann Lee."

Everyone looked at Ann Lee and for a brief moment she withered inside. She was glad she did not hold their attention long.

"Our kids are bright," Mr. Harbisson said, "but they're not intellectuals. Sure, they aren't challenged around here, but the point is they don't want to be challenged."

"I think Tucker would have stayed on at Saint Anselm's if his best friend hadn't left," said Mrs. Harbisson.

"It's other kids who are important to them at this age," agreed Mrs. Thurman. "Maggie insisted on going out for cheerleading. I said, 'Think about your grades. Think about all those late-night games you have to go to whether you have a test to study for or not.' But she was bound and determined. Nothing we could say would stop her."

Mr. Thurman cut himself a slice of cheese and put it on a cracker. "Now she's going with this hunk on the basketball team and that's all she cares about."

"She's at East Gate, isn't she?"

"That's right."

"What can you do?" asked Mrs. Harbisson. "It's the peer group that's everything at this age. Now take Tucker—"

As if on cue, Tucker drifted in with a smile and settled in a chair near his mother.

"I thought we were going to have to send out a search party," Mrs. Harbisson said. "Maybe we can eat now."

She swept into the kitchen and in a sudden burst of activity began producing hot dishes. Mr. Harbisson moved around the table pouring the wine.

Ann Lee's place card put her next to Tucker. She stood stiffly behind her chair, dreading that dinner would be a demonstration of exactly how unimportant this particular member of Tucker's peer group was to him.

At last, slightly winded, Mrs. Harbisson sat down and urged everyone to begin. A few minutes later Tucker addressed his first words to Ann Lee. "Could you pass me the pepper, please?"

She passed the pepper and tried to remember her mother's instructions. Draw him out, her mother had said. She cleared her throat. "So, how are you liking West Mount, now that you're settled in?"

He shrugged. "I like it." For some minutes Tucker's interest in his food was uninterrupted. The adults were engrossed in a passionate discussion on the subject of leveraged buyouts. Everyone was speaking so heatedly that Ann Lee hoped no one would notice that she and Tucker had nothing to say to each other.

"But these people who do takeovers are just like the ones who do arbitrage in my book. They don't produce anything, that's my point," said Mrs. Harbisson. She looked away from the argument long enough to see one of her guests groping for the dinner rolls. "Darling," she murmured, "pass the bread tray to Mr. Turner."

Ann Lee and Tucker reflexively reached for the bread tray at the same time. Ann Lee withdrew her hand in confusion, and Tucker handed the silver bread tray down the table. Then Ann Lee realized that her napkin had slipped to the floor. She bent down as discreetly as possible, only to encounter Tucker's hand. He was reaching beneath the table for his own napkin.

"This one's mine, I think." He smiled at her. "Hey, weren't you sitting at the lunch table I was at the other day?"

Ann Lee colored, mortified. He hadn't even recognized her. How incredibly insignificant she must be if she could sit through an entire lunch period with somebody and have him not recognize her. "Yes," she said faintly.

"That crowd of yours is kind of cliquish, isn't it?"

"Oh, I don't know. We just eat lunch together. We got in the habit back when we had assigned seating and I guess we never got out of it."

"I had an idea you weren't too anxious for anybody new to sit with you."

"Oh, no, I'm sure you're imagining that. In fact, didn't I see Rainey wave to you?"

"Well, but Blake made a crack or two."

"You must have misunderstood or something. It's really not that way at all. I mean, sometimes we all sit with other people and, my gosh, Blake's nice to everybody."

With a sense of desperation, Ann Lee saw that Tucker had thrust his fork into a nest of poppy seed noodles and was looking away from her. She cleared her throat. "Of course—" she began.

He glanced at her, and she went on quickly in a low voice. "It might be that Blake is jealous or something."

He looked pleased. "Nah, you think that? Why would he be jealous?"

"Well, I think he's got this thing for Rainey. Maybe he didn't like it that she sort of encouraged you to come over. That's just a guess, you understand."

"Blake and Rainey? You're putting me on."

Ann Lee felt almost drunk with the unaccustomed sensation that she was making a hit. He was listening to her closely now. "I'm serious," she said. "The other day Blake thought Susan was saying something bad about Rainey and he squirted her in the face with a hose. Honestly!"

"No joke. But is that all there is to it? I mean, maybe the hose thing was an accident or something."

Ann Lee thought desperately. "Well, this fall, when

Blake got his Corvette, he more or less gave his old car to Rainey. Maybe she gave him ten dollars or something. He just really likes her.''

"That was when he got his Corvette, huh?"

Ann Lee nodded.

"I don't get it," Tucker said. "If Blake has got this thing for Rainey, why hasn't he gone after her? They don't go together, do they?"

Ann Lee had admitted that they didn't.

"It doesn't make any sense. She wouldn't just brush off a guy like Blake. Are you sure about this?"

Ann Lee nodded vigorously.

"So what's going on?"

She whispered, "I think it's just now dawning on him how he feels. He's very out of touch with his feelings. Susan explained all that to me once. She took a psychology course, you know."

Tucker had slipped down a little in his chair. He was looking faintly amused. "Well, that's interesting. Very interesting."

Ann Lee's eyes were on his face trying to determine if his smile was friendly or not. She hoped she hadn't said something that sounded stupid. "So what kind of thing are you writing for *Endnotes*?"

"A short story, I guess." He fiddled absently with the salt shaker until his mother shot him a look and he hastily put it down.

"I'm doing a series of comic poems," Ann Lee said. "I hope one of them gets picked for the magazine."

"I thought everybody's stuff got put in."

"Well, mostly, I guess. But Blake is supposed to edit it."

"Oh, right. I guess he would." This time the sardonic

note in Tucker's voice was unmistakable, but Ann Lee wasn't sure what to make of it.

"So I suppose he'll pick and choose, you know, keeping in mind what space they have and everything."

Their conversation trailed off. Ann Lee didn't care. She had the feeling she had acquitted herself rather well. Anybody who had glanced over at them would have seen that the two of them had talked, that Tucker had even looked entertained. She decided that she had not done at all badly considering that Tucker wasn't even sure who she was.

Six

Blake felt unaccountably uncomfortable. It was all Tucker's fault, he thought resentfully. Everything had been fine until Tucker came along stirring things up. The worst part was, he admitted to himself, that there was no reason Rainey shouldn't go out with Tucker. She probably would. Blake had seen any number of girls fall for that guy's smarmy charm. During the summer Tucker spent a lot of time hanging around the country club swimming pool. From the tennis courts Blake could see him rubbing suntan lotion on one girl after another. Once, when Blake had been on his way to the snack bar, he glanced over at the pool and saw Tucker moving through the water with a long-legged brunette riding on his shoulders.

But then he had to admit that he had never liked Tucker. He disliked the way Tucker looked on the world as nothing but one big party. It offended Blake's personal code. He did think his parents were too hung up on achievement, but he also felt that a guy ought to do something serious with his life. Tucker was the kind of guy who should have worn a T-shirt saying "Life is a Beach." It summed him up completely.

Blake didn't believe that Rainey was mixed up with either Tucker or drugs. But the power of suggestion is so strong that once Susan had brought the question up, he didn't feel quite easy in his mind. He decided it was as if someone has told you not to think of a blue polar bear. As soon as he's said it you catch yourself continually thinking about blue polar bears. The more he reminded himself that there was nothing to the things Susan had said, the more uneasy he felt.

What happened Monday morning didn't make him feel any better.

Blake came up behind Rainey at the lockers and she jumped half out of her skin. "Sorry," he said. "I didn't mean to do that to you." He pulled his books out of the locker and glanced at her. "Is everything okay?"

The blood seemed to drain from her face. Her dark eyes looked as if they were staring out from behind a mask. "Everything's fine. Why do people keep asking me that?"

Blake leaned a shoulder against his locker, wondering why she was so shaken. "Who's asking you?"

"First Mrs. Armstrong and now you—that's two." Rainey threw her algebra book in the locker, and slammed the thin metal door so it shuddered violently. "It's starting to get to me. I'm just a little tired of cold weather, a little ready for spring, a little overworked—is that a crime?" She turned away abruptly.

When she reached the walkway, her black hair turned to

fire for a second in the sunlight, and Blake felt his heart turn over. She seemed so small and vulnerable that he wanted to run after her and tell her that whatever it was he would make it all right.

He frowned at his locker. Something was wrong. Rainey was not the type to fall to pieces over nothing. It was too much of a coincidence, Susan gossiping about Rainey and then this. Something must be going on.

That afternoon Blake had to go to the library to work on a history paper, but he found that he couldn't stop thinking about Rainey. He knew he could concentrate on history if he cleared up the question of what was bothering her. He went over to the metal filing cabinets where the library kept ordinance survey maps of the county, found one of the area near the city limits north of town, and took it back to a dark corner of the library where he knew he wouldn't be interrupted. He spread the map out and studied it. It was not up to date. The Starlight Trailer Park, for example, had been built since it had been printed. But it was not difficult to find the dirt road that ran past the old farmhouse where Jesse lived. The scale of the map was so large that the shape of Jesse's house was clearly outlined as were some sheds and outbuildings at the back of the McCracken's lot. Blake knew the trailer park had to be almost directly across the dirt road in front of the house. After a few minutes he pinpointed the tobacco barn. The map even showed in dotted lines traces of an old road that had run behind the tobacco barn before it became overgrown.

He looked at the map, puzzled. It was hard to come up with a reason for Rainey's being in that pasture by the tobacco barn. The barn was a fair distance from the trailer park. A country road went behind the pasture but there was no earthly reason Rainey would have parked on that back road and made her way across a quarter of mile of rough pasture land when a more convenient road ran up to her door. It was odd, all right. No doubt there was some perfectly innocent explanation, but it was hard for him to imagine what it could be.

He packed up all his books and papers and left the library. For once, looking at his long, lean car didn't flood his senses with satisfaction. The problem with a red car, he decided, was that it could be seen for miles. And it was like a calling card. Practically anybody who saw it would recognize it as his. He needed a less conspicuous car.

Blake didn't stop to analyze why he was doing what he was doing. If he tried to put the reason into words, he might have to face some things he wasn't ready to face.

When he got home, he banged the kitchen door closed behind him. ''Mom? I want to take your car out for a while, okay?''

Mrs. Farraby stopped with her wooden spoon poised in midair. ''Wait a minute, why do you want my car? What exactly do you have in mind?''

''Don't worry, I'm not going to hurt it. It's just that, well, I just washed the Vette.''

''You've got to get it dirty sometime, sweetie. You can't keep a car in a plastic bag.''

''I know, but—can't I just borrow yours for now?''

She resumed her attack on the batter in the bowl. ''All right, I guess so. I'll cause quite a sensation driving up to White's in the Corvette, but I suppose I can put up with it.''

Ordinarily, the idea of his mother taking his car to the grocery store would have made Blake's blood run cold, but he couldn't worry about that right now.

''Just be careful with it, okay?'' he pleaded. ''Don't let some nut bang one of those stupid carts into it.''

64

She bowed sardonically as he backed out of the kitchen.

He grabbed the keys to the new station wagon off the key holder and was out the door in a flash. When he got the station wagon out on the road he gritted his teeth. He hated its spongy steering, its sloppy brakes, and the slab of a seat that felt like a couch. But he had to force himself to concentrate on navigating because he wasn't perfectly familiar with the area of town where Rainey and Jesse lived. He had been out to Jesse's house only a few times, but luckily the map he had studied in the library was still fresh in his mind. Once he reached the city limits it didn't take him long to find the dirt road he was looking for. He turned onto the country road that ran behind the McCrackens' land, then he slowed and started watching for the tobacco barn. When he spotted it, he could hardly believe he had the right place. He had imagined the barn shown on the map to be an ordinary building, but this place, with its caved-in roof, its decayed wood and a few strips of tar paper hanging forlornly on the north side, was less like a building than a blown mushroom. It was actually falling down.

He parked among a bunch of trees, got out of the car, and looked around. Some young cows were clustered around a feed trough at the other end of the pasture. Blake was relieved to note that none of them had horns. After a moment's hesitation he climbed through the rusty barbed wire fence that encircled the pasture. To his relief, the cows were so intent on their food they didn't seem to notice him. He picked his way through the rough grass hoping he wouldn't get a load of buckshot in his rear. He felt uneasy poking around on other people's property.

When he reached the other side and looked up, he was startled to see a man not ten feet ahead of him. He took an involuntary step backward and froze. The man had appeared from nowhere. Blake supposed he had come up by way of the woods, but if so, he had been strangely quiet about it. Blake had heard no crashing through the underbrush and no snapping twigs.

The stranger struck a match on the sole of his shoe and lit a cigarette. "Nice weather for a walk." He had a low, lazy voice, but what was so unusual about him was the gypsy look of his tangled curly black hair.

"Yeah, it's starting to warm up." Blake cleared his throat and plunged his hands into his pockets. "Do you live around here?"

"Yeah. What about you?" The man's black eyes met his so directly that Blake could feel hot color rise to his cheeks. The remark made him acutely aware of his trespasser status, but he couldn't believe this fellow owned this property. If anybody owned it, it had to be Jesse McCracken's family.

"I'm just looking around," said Blake with all the firmness he could muster. Something was off about this guy, he thought. The flat *i* in *nice* marked him as a native. But shoulder-length hair was uncommon among country people around here. And without being entirely conscious of it, Blake was vaguely aware that the farmers in his part of the world tended to be blond or a kind of milky brunette.

The stranger blew a smoke ring and they both watched as it floated, then faded into air.

Blake felt uncomfortably aware of the stranger's calm. He began to wish he had never come poking around, but he forced himself to say something. "So, uh, where do you live? A friend of mine lives in that farmhouse over there."

"Oh, down the road a piece." The man jerked his head to indicate the woods behind him.

Blake knew that nothing was past the woods except the trailer park and a dead-end dirt road. Of course, it was pos-

66

sible that the guy lived in the trailer park, but that still didn't explain what he was doing on the McCrackens' land. Blake had no idea whether drugs or something shady like that was part of the picture, but he almost didn't care. He began to feel profoundly uneasy. More important, he felt silly. Suddenly he couldn't imagine what had possessed him to come tromping around this pasture. He needed a way to leave without its being obvious that he was turning tail and running. "Well, I'll see you," he said awkwardly as he backed away.

The dark stranger's face broke into a network of lines when he smiled and Blake had a peculiar shock of recognition. "Do you——" he began. "Oh, never mind." He turned around and began walking quickly back to his car. The young cows at the other end of the pasture had turned around and were making noises that were somewhere between a bleat and a moo. Blake was anxious to get out of there before he had to cope with a stampede or something. All the while he walked back across the pasture, the skin between his shoulder blades felt tight.

When he got back to the station wagon, he glanced back across the field to the tobacco barn. The stranger had disappeared.

Blake was pretty sure he knew now what was going on, but the whole incident had been so peculiar it was almost unreal. He felt stupid and out of his element. He got in the station wagon and pulled out onto the country road. Then he spotted a familiar car approaching. It was a car no one could mistake. It's chassis had a shapeless quality and its paint job was the color and consistency of peanut butter. He would have known it anywhere. He had sold it to Rainey in the fall. When he passed the car, he looked in and saw Rainey. When she met his eyes, a look of shock passed over her face. She had obviously not expected to see him in that car. More important, she had not expected to see him there, on that road. He looked in the rearview mirror and watched as her car slowed and pulled into the trees to park. She must have been pretty shaken. It would have made better sense for her to drive on past the pasture and pretend she had nothing to do with the tobacco barn. Blake drove on and turned onto the first road thinking hard.

He was reasonably sure that the man at the tobacco barn had to be Rainey's dad. For a second back by the barn he had seen Rainey in the stranger's eyes. It was not a strong likeness, but it was there in the smile, the eyes, and the eyebrows.

His mind brimmed with wild conjectures. Once Rainey saw her father, she was bound to find out that Blake had talked to him. What was going to happen then? Blake didn't even know what he wanted to happen. He was pretty sure he didn't want Rainey admitting to him that she was harboring her father. That would make him an accomplice after the fact. Mr. Locklear was wanted by the police, after all. It might be better if she didn't tell him anything. But he wondered if he should warn her that Jesse had seen her in the pasture.

Blake got no work done on his history paper that evening and the next morning at school all he could think about was Rainey. He kept a sharp eye out for her, but she seemed to have disappeared. For an awful minute, he found himself thinking that she had gone away with her father and that he would never see her again. But when he went into creative writing class she was sitting at her usual desk. He tried to catch her eye, but she looked away from him.

He wasn't sure what he'd say to her when he got a chance to speak to her. He only wanted to let her know he hadn't called the police. After all, he told himself, he didn't know for sure that the man at the barn was Rainey's father. He only suspected it. He wasn't obliged to go to the police purely on the basis of an apparent resemblance between Rainey and some man he had seen at the tobacco barn.

When the bell rang after class, he bolted after her, but there was a bottleneck at the door and when he succeeded in getting out of the classroom, she had disappeared. He stood there for a second, swearing softly. Why had she run off like that?

He watched for her again at lunch. His eyes checking over the whole cafeteria, but there was no sign of her.

He put his tray down next to Ann Lee's. "Have you talked to Rainey today?"

"I think so. I saw her in history. Why? Were you supposed to get something from her or what?"

"I don't know," Blake said unhappily. "It's not like her to skip lunch."

"Maybe she's dieting."

"Rainey? Dieting? Good grief, Ann Lee, she doesn't need to diet. You're out of your mind."

"Maybe she had to study for a test, maybe she went home sick."

"Maybe she's avoiding me," he said flatly.

"Why would she be doing that?"

The way Ann Lee was looking at him made him sorry that he'd said anything. He shrugged. Michael came over and began to go into a long tale of woe about how he was afraid Cynthia was going to get the job she had applied for in Virginia. Under the circumstances, Blake found it very hard to keep his attention on Michael's troubles.

He figured that after school would be his last chance. There was no point in following her to her job since he couldn't stand in the middle of the restaurant and talk about her father. And he had doubts about going over to her place.

He decided to try to catch her at her locker. Coming around the corner of A wing, he heard her voice in the confused babble that was coming from the locker alcove. "Rainey!" he yelled. A herd of kids surged out of the locker alcove. Blake's head snapped around checking among them for Rainey, but there was no sign of her. After the kids passed, the only person left in the locker alcove was a guy with purple hair who was stuffing some smelly tennis shoes into his locker with what looked like a week's worth of laundry.

"Have you seen Rainey?"

The boy stared at him blankly. He was skinny and had major complexion problems.

"Do you know who I'm talking about?" demanded Blake.

The boy with the purple hair turned and walked away without a word.

Watching him leave, Blake had a strong impulse to grab him and shake him until he talked. He took a deep breath to steady himself. "Jeez, a guy could get paranoid," he muttered. He looked around the locker alcove in some confusion. He was sure he had heard Rainey's voice yet he hadn't seen her come out of the alcove. Where could she have gone? Had he hallucinated her voice or something?

Suddenly he heard a noise and wheeled around. Listening hard, he heard the familiar sounds of voices out on the walkway and the groan of the school bus motors in the distance, but the sound he heard had been different from that. It was a metal sound and close at hand. Yet nothing was behind him. Just the lockers. He noticed something odd, though. Rainey's locker didn't have its combination lock on it.

Blake jerked the locker open, and there was Rainey.

"Good God!" Blaked stared at her, aghast.

She was scrunched up in her locker like a mummy with her elbows in front of her and her hands pressed on either side of her face. She looked as if she was going to cry. She hiccuped, then half wiggled, half fell out of the locker.

Blake grabbed her shoulders. "What are you doing in there, Rainey? What if you'd suffocated, for Pete's sake?"

"The locker has ventilation slits," she pointed out with dignity.

"What's going on? Why did you skip lunch? Why did you jump inside your locker when you heard me coming? Do you have to act like I'm some kind of monster or something?"

She sniffled. "Leave me alone."

Blake could hardly believe what he was about to say, but he choked it out. "Maybe I could help you." His mouth felt dry.

"I don't want your help. *Leave me alone!*" In a sudden movement, Rainey wrenched herself out of his hands and ran out.

Blake stood there for several seconds, swearing. A sense of his own powerlessness had come over him suddenly and he felt sick.

SEVEN

W hy are you getting all dressed up just to meet Ann Lee at the mall?'' asked Mrs. Brantley.

"I'm not all dressed up.'' Susan smoothed her mushroom-colored eye shadow with her little finger. "Besides, Mom, everybody's at the mall on Saturday night. I can't go looking like a slob.''

"I don't understand the way kids run in packs these days. When I was your age, boys used to come to the door and call on a girl.''

"They still do, Mom. Sometimes. I'm just between boys right now.''

"Not that I want you to get all involved with someone at your age. It's good for you to develop your own interests and to be independent. I'm glad that you're not one of those boy-crazy types. I just wonder what happened to all those nice boys who used to come around taking you to dances and parties."

"They'll probably be at the mall tonight."

Mrs. Brantley frowned. "Not that a woman's value depends on what men think of her."

Susan was accustomed to this tangle of contradictory remarks from her mother. It was as if some formative time in her life Mrs. Brantley had been at a NOW meeting, but had spent the time serving cookies. She couldn't decide whether Susan should be a supreme court justice or the most popular girl in the eleventh grade. Susan only hoped that her mother's internal conflicts over the proper role of women in society would keep her so distracted that she wouldn't start asking intelligent questions. Clearly she had already noticed that Susan's entire pattern of behavior had changed. But she attributed the change to broad sociological forces. She didn't have a clue about the true reason.

Susan glanced at her watch. "Oh, my gosh! I've got to go."

"Well, while you're out there, would you pick up a package of light bulbs? Oh, yes, and a new cuttlebone for the bird. You won't forget, will you?"

"Light bulbs. Cuttlebone. Check."

When Susan got to the mall, Jesse was waiting for her. He sat at a Formica table near a palm tree. She mimed an enthusiastic greeting from the door, waving both hands. Grinning, he jumped up and ran to meet her. They held each other's hands and whirled round and round on the terrazzo floor. "Motorboat, motorboat, go so fast," sang Susan. "Motorboat, motorboat, step on the gas!" Jesse grabbed her from behind and lifted her up off the floor.

"Okay, lady," he said gruffly. "Where to from here?"

"Some place private," she said. "As agreed."

"Your mother didn't think it was funny that you left for the movie so early?"

"My mother doesn't think. She just worries. She did ask me tonight whatever happened to all those nice boys who used to come around."

Jesse put her down abruptly. "Jeez, Susan. It stinks."

"Don't start on that. Please! You're going to ruin the whole evening. All I see is that we've got kind of a compromise in a sticky situation, all right? Let's get something to eat."

He frowned as he took out his car keys. "You like Chinese?"

"Like, I *love* Chinese. In a former life my name was Mai Ling Ling."

"You sure it wasn't Mai Ding-a-Ling? You're a nut."

"You love me, though, don't you?"

"You bet I do." He swatted her playfully on the bottom as they headed out to the car.

Jesse's attraction for Susan was so strong that he felt that his love was like a magnificent natural force—it could have lit a city block. He couldn't figure out why a comparatively little thing, like the fact that he had to see Susan behind her parents' backs, got to him so much. But it made him feel dirty. Almost as if he were losing part of who he was.

At the Shanghai Express the dining area was done up like old-fashioned train compartments. Susan and Jesse found a table at the very end of the dark compartment. Their booth had a little window with a green fringed window shade pulled down to conceal the fact that it was only a wall on the other side of the train window and not the Chinese countryside whizzing past. The table was lit by a tiny red and green paneled lantern. "I'll have the moo goo gai pan and an egg roll.'' Susan folded the shiny red menu and handed it back to the waitress.

After Jesse gave her his order, the waitress, a bouffant blond in a Chinese shift, took the menu and minced away down the dark passageway.

Susan spread her fingers out on the table. Her rings gleamed in the dim light and her pale face seemed to swim in the darkness. Jesse almost felt dizzy with the longing to touch her.

''We'll pretend we're on a train in China.'' She smiled at him. ''Do you want to be the Russian spy, or should I?''

''You be the spy.'' Jesse reached for her hand and brushed it against his lips.

''You'd better not get cozy with a Russian spy. The next thing you know you'll be telling her all your secrets.''

''I don't care. It's too late for me. I'm a lost soul. Susan, what are we going to do about the prom?''

Her hand jerked. ''I thought we weren't going to talk about that.''

''Don't you figure we'll still be going together then?''

''Of course we'll still be going together!''

''And don't you want to go to the prom? Isn't that the kind of thing you practically live for? Are you figuring you'll stay home or go with some other guy or what?''

''I'm not thinking about it. We'll work out something. That's months from now.''

''You know, it's not as if I'm some kind of criminal or something. What could your father say except that he hates my father's guts?''

''You don't have to live with Daddy. I do. You wouldn't believe what it's like when he gets a certain mind-set about something. Like, when I was in the third grade he said we should have a rock garden in the backyard. Mom said she didn't *want* a rock garden, but the next thing she knows a crane drops this five hundred-pound rock in the backyard, then a backhoe comes in and scrapes away a quarter of the backyard. We went to Maine for vacation that year and we had to come back with our suitcases full of *rocks*. Now our backyard looks like the surface of the moon.

"Your dad has real talent for ruining neighborhoods."

"Don't start on Dad," she pleaded.

"I was just agreeing with you. You started it."

"I'm only trying to explain why I don't want to come up against him."

"Look, think about it for a minute. You really believe we can go on like this without him finding out about it?"

"The places Dad goes—like Rotary Club meetings and Chamber of Commerce meetings and stuff—they don't sit around talking about us. I'm pretty sure of that."

"That shows how much you know. Besides, even if nobody says anything to your dad, somebody's bound to let on to your mother sooner or later."

"I've thought about that. But I'm not sure Mom would pass it on to Daddy even if she knew. She doesn't want to have the roof blow off the house any more than I do."

"But look at it this way. If your parents catch you sneaking around they've really got something on you. Then they can say you've been lying, you've been sneaking off. They'll have a good reason for grounding you for the rest of your natural life."

"My dad doesn't go in for grounding. He goes in for scenes, indigestion, and everybody having crying jags while he yells. I don't want to give him any excuse. Come on, do we have to borrow trouble? Can't we just enjoy what we've got?"

She tweaked his nose and he found himself grinning reluctantly.

"Stop being so gloomy."

"Moo goo gai pan?" asked the waitress in a nasal whine.

"Here," said Susan promptly.

When the waitress had set down their orders and left, Susan leaned over the table and said, "It's going to be all right, Jesse. I love you and you love me. What else can matter?"

He had to be satisfied with that.

After what had happened at the locker alcove, Blake knew better than to try to talk to Rainey. She was obviously ready to take extreme measures to avoid seeing him and he was afraid if he pushed her to talk to him, she might end up doing something desperate like diving out a window, which was the last thing he wanted.

He had been thinking of almost nothing but Rainey and her dad for days. Mr. Locklear had been gone for years. Why should he come home now? He obviously wasn't trying to reconcile with Rainey's mother. He couldn't have come to take Rainey away, either, because days had passed and Rainey was still around. And Blake only had to look at her face to realize that her father was still around, too. Why? It was barely possible he was planning some wild and illegal political action, but Blake didn't think so. Mr. Locklear wouldn't hang around Rainey if he were planning anything dangerous. And if he were just hiding out, with no particular plans, it made sense for him to do it somewhere else. The world was full of places in which it was easier to hide out than a town where your face had been splashed all over the newspapers. Blake hadn't recognized Rainey's father because he had been pretty young when the mess had blown up. People who had been grown-up then, particularly people who had know Locklear, would be sure to recognize him.

The more Blake thought about it, the more he came to one conclusion—Rainey's dad had probably come home to get money and Rainey hadn't been able to get it for him yet. Where would she get it? She'd only just finished paying Blake off for the car he had sold her at the rate of ten dollars a payday. She obviously was chronically short of cash, like everybody else Blake knew. Maybe more short than most.

No matter which way he examined it, the conclusion seemed inescapable. What Rainey needed was money. Put that way, the problem seemed fairly simple. Even solvable.

At lunch the next day Blake sat with Ann Lee again. He had the faint hope that force of habit would eventually bring Rainey back to her old table. But he had to watch helplessly as she carried her tray to a far corner of the cafeteria and sat down next to Crash Wukolski. Even from this distance, he could see Crash's ears turning a dull raspberry red.

"Did you and Rainey have a fight?" Ann Lee looked at him curiously.

"No."

"I didn't even know she knew Crash Wukolski. I mean, I'm sure he's very nice, but he's so shy. As far as I know he's never even talked to a girl. Where's Michael?"

"Back over at the hospital, crying onto his whole wheat and alfalfa sprouts, I guess." Blake tore his roll apart and looked at it in disgust. "He spends months telling Cynthia she ought not to put up with all that junk at the hospital, then when she takes his advice and starts looking for another job he falls apart. People are nuts."

"You may be right about that," Ann Lee said diplomatically.

Tucker pulled out a chair and sat down. "Hi, guys."

"Hi, Tucker." Ann Lee smiled. "How are you?"

"Where's Rainey?" he asked.

Blake indicated the far corner of the cafeteria.

"No joke." Tucker peered in that direction with interest. "Is she going with that guy?"

"I don't think so." Ann Lee cast an anxious look at Blake.

"Glad to hear it. I swear the guy looks like part of some prehistoric exhibit—Man at the Dawn of Time. Well, is she going with anybody?"

"What do you care?" Blake ripped his milk carton open. "That's never stopped you before."

"True." Tucker smiled. "You know, if you don't mind, I think I'll just go over there and join them."

Blake watched Tucker make his way through the cafeteria tables. He hoped to have the pleasure of seeing Tucker slip on a discarded french fry, but no such luck. Instead, Blake had the painful experience of seeing Rainey look up at him with pleased surprise.

She was glad to see Tucker, Blake thought bitterly, because Tucker was too dim to suspect anything was going on. And because he didn't know her well enough or care enough about her to realize she was coming unglued. It was a crazy world, a world where things worked exactly opposite to the way any reasonable person would expect. Blake had noticed it before, but it had never struck him with such bitter force.

"Crash could cream Tucker if he wanted to." Ann Lee leaned her chin on her hand and looked almost wistful. Who would have suspected that Ann Lee's placid exterior concealed a primitive blood lust? But Tucker could do that to a person.

"Nobody will ever cream Tucker." Blake turned away. He didn't want to have to watch the happy little party of three. "He's the kind that's slippery when wet."

*   *   *

"Tucker!" Rainey exclaimed when he sat down at her table. "Hi!"

"Hi, there."

"Do you know Crash Wukolski?"

"Pleased to meet you, Crash."

Crash grunted. He was a massive boy with a muscular neck and small but expressive brown eyes.

"I was just explaining to Crash how our writing class is going to have a bake sale Saturday to raise money for *Endnotes*."

Tucker buttered a roll. "He could be our first customer. Something tells me you love to eat, right, Crash?"

Crash's eyes instantly seemed to develop red veins. Tucker prudently backed his chair away from the table a little.

"We're borrowing the home ec kitchen," Rainey put in. "Saturday morning we're going to bake fresh bread and brownies and cookies and then we'll sell them at the mall."

"We'll make a mint."

Rainey bit into her sandwich. "You'll have to come by the mall at lunch and try some of our stuff, Crash."

"It's going to be positively delish!" Tucker grinned.

"Have you finished your story yet, Tucker?"

"I've got the rough draft done. It's going to be a sensitive, yet poignant tale of a junior who comes to a strange school and loses his heart to a petite, exotic beauty who doesn't know he's alive. I think at the conclusion I'm going to have him end it all by diving off the second story of A wing."

"I hate stories with sad endings." Rainey looked at him under her lashes.

"You'll have to give me a new ending then. What's your story like?"

"It's a horror story. It's about a blob that lives on human flesh."

"No joke! Gee, I love that kind of story. Did you see *The Fly*? Too bad the sequel wasn't as good as the original. You know, the trouble is that nowadays all you seem to get are these butcher movies. I mean, anybody can go to a slaughterhouse, buy a few hundred pounds of raw sausage and spill it all over a set, right? That is not art."

"You need psychological suspense," agreed Rainey.

"Right. I absolutely agree. It's not what you see, it's what you imagine that gets to you. I like it when you get some kind of insight into the monster's mind. You know, the tragedy of being ugly and grotesque, that kind of thing."

"I can see you're a real fan of the genre."

"Isn't that what I'm telling you?"

Rainey was a little surprised she could like someone so different from herself, but she saw now that Tucker had all the parts that were missing from herself. They would be a perfect couple, a kind of yin and yang making an ideal whole. She loved his light manner, the smoothness of his fair hair, and the vague aura of privilege that clung to his expensive clothes. He seemed to come from a world that floated above the dark and dusty one where she was desperately struggling to raise two hundred dollars.

"Tell you what," he said. "Why don't I come pick you up for the bake thing Saturday morning."

"Do you know where I live? It's not exactly on your way."

"Draw me a map."

"Okay."

She began sketching on a napkin with light pencil marks. She felt uncomfortable drawing the map. In her mind it seemed dangerously close to being a map of how to get to the tobacco barn, though she was careful to leave out the country road that ran behind the pasture.

She still hadn't figured out what had led Blake to go poking around back there, but seeing him there had made her feel exposed. It was like being in one of those awful dreams, she thought, the ones where you imagine yourself being in church naked.

Her father had argued that Blake obviously knew nothing, but he didn't seem to grasp how odd the whole thing was. Blake wasn't the sort who took long walks in the country, and that field was miles from his house. He obviously had to know something or he wouldn't have been there in the first place. But what did he suspect? What did he know? Wondering about it was driving her crazy. Yet she was afraid if she tried to find out exactly what he did know, she might end up telling Blake everything. Whenever she caught a glimpse of him, she got the awful sensation she was about to blurt out the whole truth.

"Now what's this big road here?" Tucker asked.

Rainey was startled. "Uh—that? That's Greenacre Road. You, uh, pass a convenience store about here." She marked an X on the napkin. "You sure this isn't going to be too much trouble?"

"Nah." He smiled a golden smile at her and for a giddy instant it seemed as if a normal life was within her reach— going out with a boy, going to a school event, just like any girl might. She smiled back at him, enjoying the moment more than she would have thought possible. She liked Tucker. Tucker felt safe.

Eight

_L_ook, I just want to warn you," Ann Lee told Susan, "that you'd better not tell your mom you're meeting me at the mall this Friday because I'm going to that missionary supper at church with my parents and your mom is bound to see me there because she's serving coffee."

"Oh, no! Do you _have_ to go to the dumb supper?"

"Come on, Susan. It may not be as exciting as your social life, but it's all I've got. I mean, actual boys go to those things. Sometimes they even talk to me. It has happened. You can't expect me to sit home so you can go out with Jesse."

"I know, I know, but— You can't do this to me! Not this Friday! Jesse's got tickets to a dinner theatre show in Raleigh and they cost him a fortune."

"Just tell your mom you're going with somebody else. I don't see the problem."

Susan threw herself down on her bed. "I don't know," she whimpered. "The truth is this whole situation is getting messy. Saturday night I forgot to get a couple of dumb things Mom asked me to pick up at the mall and she started asking me all these questions, like, how could I be at the mall for hours and hours and forget to pick up cuttlebone? As if anybody could remember something as stupid as cuttlebone! I told her that most of the time we had been in the movie and if you can believe it, she started asking me questions about the *movie*!"

"You and Jesse didn't end up going to the movie?"

"Of course we went to the movie but we took so long over dinner and we got there late so I never really did figure out what was going on and I wasn't paying all that much attention, to tell you the truth."

"I guess not." Having seen the way Susan and Jesse acted with each other in the school cafeteria, Ann Lee could guess what they'd be like in a dark movie theatre.

"The point is, she's getting suspicious! She asks me what happened to all the boys I used to know. She's started peering into my eyes and asking me weird questions like she thinks maybe I'm sneaking away to do drugs. I don't know. I've got to *do* something. What if she says something to Daddy? I'll just *die!*"

Ann Lee was ashamed to admit to herself that she took just the tiniest bit of satisfaction in Susan's distress. But even if she wasn't in her heart as sympathetic as she should have been, she could at least give herself full marks for not saying "I told you so."

Susan covered her eyes with her arm and snuffled. "Do you think maybe Jesse's right and it's all going to blow up in my face any day? Tell me the truth."

Ann Lee patted her awkwardly on the shoulder. "Oh,

it'll be all right. You'll think of something. Don't worry.''

''Why does my father have to be so *weird?* Nobody else has to live like this. Whoever heard of a feud in modern times? I tell you, Ann Lee, I hope I do get that summer abroad thing because I don't know how much more of this I can take.'' Susan wiped the back of her hand across her nose.

''Want me to get you an aspirin?''

Susan turned facedown on the pillow and wailed. ''No! I want you to get me a whole new family! A whole new life!''

After Blake pulled his car up into the driveway that afternoon, he fished his wallet out of his pocket and checked to make sure that the crisp one hundred dollar bill he had just withdrawn from the bank was still there.

All afternoon he'd been thinking about Rusty, the dog he'd had when he was a kid. It was probably taking the hundred dollars out of the bank that had done it because Rusty had kept Blake broke all the time. An Irish setter, he had the habit of retreiving anything the neighbors left outside. He would come home with one muddy shoe, a golf sock, a Raggedy Ann doll. He must have taken his trophies swimming because generally they didn't look like much once he got them home, and Blake's parents not only made him return everything and apologize, they made him pay for anything that had been ruined. Blake still remembered the time Rusty was spotted swiping a huge sirloin fresh off the grill. That had wiped out two weeks' allowance.

Irish setters are not generally thought of as the intellectuals of the dog world, but Rusty was smart. He could climb out of the fenced backyard and he could dig under it as well, which was how he managed to get into so much trouble. He knew how to shake hands and he always got off Blake's bed as soon as he heard Mrs. Farraby's footsteps.

When Rusty got old he started tripping over his feet. His breath smelled bad, and he couldn't see too well, either. Blake had to give him medicine three times a day, help him up and down off the bed, and clean up his messes. The odd thing was that the more time he spent taking care of Rusty, the more he felt he could never get along without him. After Rusty died, he never wanted another pet. Rusty couldn't be replaced, and Blake hadn't wanted to feel that aching grief again.

Now, as he touched the crisp hundred dollar bill, he had the sensation that he was falling into a trap he had long avoided. He felt the tugging on his heart, the uncomfortable mixed feeling of responsibility and of helplessness that he remembered from those days when he had Rusty. He dimly sensed he was making a mistake, but he couldn't stop himself. He had to help Rainey.

So far she had avoided him, but they were going to be together at the bake sale Saturday morning and he'd have the chance to get her alone then and give her the money.

Susan had been watching for Blake from her bedroom window. As soon as she saw his car pull into the driveway, she put on her sister's sweat suit, jogged around the block to the door of Farraby's house and rang the doorbell. Blake whipped the door open almost at once, but was visibly disappointed to see her. "Oh, it's you."

Susan was too preoccupied with her own troubles to be upset by his greeting. "Blake, can I talk to you for a minute? This is a little too tricky a subject to talk about over the phone. I was afraid my mom or my sister might pick up on the extension."

He looked alarmed. Glancing quickly behind him, he said, "My mom's home. We can't talk here."

Susan thrust her fists in her pockets, which made her oversize jogging pants sag alarmingly. "Maybe we could go for a ride or something."

"Okay." Blake disappeared for a minute, then returned jangling his car keys. "Let's go."

They had scarcely pulled away from the house when he said abruptly, "Okay, out with it!"

Susan looked at him in surprise. She would have thought that Blake was the one who was on edge instead of her. "Well, you know how I've been going out with Jesse," she began.

The street was wet and the Corvette was getting splashed with dirty water, but Blake seemed not to notice. He looked at her blankly. "Yeah, so what?"

Susan spoke in a rush. "Would you come by the house and pretend to take me out Friday night?"

"What? Oh, for the love of—"

"Just do me this one little favor, Blake. All you have to do is come by the house and take me to the mall. Drive me one way, that's all. I'll fake the coming home part. Jesse can let me out at the corner."

"You're out of your mind."

"It's only a *little* favor, and the day may come when you'll want me to do you a favor, you know."

Blake hesitated. He thought about how Susan knew about Rainey being seen in Jesse's back pasture. With any luck, Susan and Jesse were the only ones who did know about it. Maybe it wouldn't be such a bad idea to have the two of them owing him. He bit his lip. "Okay."

"You will! Oh, Blake! I'll never forget this! Really." Susan pecked him on the cheek.

Blake rubbed the lipstick off with the heel of his hand. "Okay, okay. Just remember, you owe me one, okay?"

Susan shrugged. "Sure. I already said that. Great."

At Susan's suggestion, Blake dropped her off at her house before going home. Mrs. Brantley was sweeping the front steps when Susan climbed out of the Corvette.

Her mother stared "I thought you went jogging."

Susan waved cheerfully as Blake drove off. "I did. But I ran into Blake and he gave me a ride home." Everything was going even more smoothly than she had expected.

"You know, if you're going to take up jogging, you're going to need to get your own sweat suit. Sandy's not going to want you getting hers sweaty all the time."

Susan untied the kerchief from around her forehead. Unlike her younger sister, she was no athlete. She thought jogging clothes were hideous and she wouldn't have dreamed of letting anybody but Blake see her in them. "I haven't quite made up my mind about whether I'm going to keep on jogging." Her mother had swallowed her story whole. At last, she thought, she was getting the break she deserved.

Friday night, Blake went by Susan's to pick her up. He had even gone to the trouble to put on his good blazer and his new shoes. He stood in the living room and made excruciatingly boring small talk with Mr. and Mrs. Brantley. "Yeah, I think winter's just about finished." "Yup, Duke has had a real good year." "I don't know what I think about those sanctions." "What do you think, Mr. Brantley?" "I'm sure you must be right, Mr. Brantley."

When Susan came downstairs with her fingernails painted to match her dress and her lips painted to match her fingernails, Blake tried to look appreciative. He sensed that he was getting drawn in deeper and deeper, but he didn't care. It was, he thought, kind of what it must be like to drink too much. By the time a person obviously had had too much, he was too far gone to have enough sense to quit.

Outside he opened the car door for Susan. He figured he might as well lay it on.

"I really appreciate this, Blake," she said once he got in. "It's going just *great*. Mom and Dad ate it up. They've always liked you."

"Just remember—"

"Right, I owe you. Just what do you have in mind, if you don't mind my asking?" She eyed him nervously. "I mean you do seem to be kind of harping on this. Not that I'm not grateful because I *am*, but—"

"Nothing in particular."

They drove in silence to the mall. Blake insisted on walking Susan from the car up to the café court inside. Jesse was at a table there, but he was sitting as if he were waiting for an invisible starting gun to fire.

"Okay," said Blake as soon as he pushed the glass doors open. "This is it. See you."

"Just remember you're at a dinner theater in Raleigh tonight," Susan said quickly. "And don't let my parents see you driving around town somewhere."

"For crying out loud, Susan!"

"And thanks!" She ran off.

Blake turned quickly and left. He had no trouble reading Jesse's face and he had no particular desire to hang around and watch someone else's humiliation. His car zipped out of the parking lot, and his arm, resting on the open window, prickled into goose bumps. A few minutes later he was speeding along the northern stretch of Greenacre Road. The Corvette's headlights shone on the rectangular white sign that said "City

Limit." Slowing the car to a crawl, he turned onto the dirt road that ran in front of Jesse's house. He soon spotted the lights of the McCrackens' big old farmhouse, which was set back from the road just a bit. Across the road purple and pink lights spelled out Starlight Trailer Park. Somebody seemed to be having a party. Muffled music was coming from a double-wide mobile home, and light and noise were spilling out its door. The dark figure of a man came wobbling out. He was making his way uncertainly to his car. Blake drove past until he was out of the range of the trailer park lights. When he got almost to the end of the dead-end road, he turned his car around. He hadn't seen Rainey's car at the trailer park, so he knew she wasn't at home, but he remembered that Michael had said her trailer was the first one on the lot. He drove slowly back, this time keeping a sharp eye on the first trailer. His headlights caught some wisps of nylon fluttering on a clothesline behind the trailer. Nobody in Blake's neighborhood had a clothesline, and he slowed down even more to look at it. He had had limited experience with women's underwear, but catching a brief glimpse of what looked like mere inches of nylon, he wondered why girls bothered to wear underwear at all if that was all there was to it. He figured you could have stored a whole set of it in a pencil case. His headlights moved across the old trailer. It was evident no one was at home. If Rainey's car had been parked in front, he might have tried to see her, but then again maybe he wouldn't have. After all, she couldn't have made it more plain that she didn't want to talk to him.

Feeling depressed, he drove home.

His mother was in the kitchen reading the evening paper. "Dad not in, yet?"

She sighed. "He was on call. Accident out on I-Ninety-five. He won't be in until pretty late."

Blake filled a glass from the ice maker and poured some strawberry seltzer over it. He let it fizz a bit because he liked it slightly flat. He looked around the great room with its fieldstone fireplace, its exposed beam ceiling, and the gleaming work island that separated all that from the stainless steel kitchen.

"Mom, have you ever thought about why we have so much more than other people?"

She folded her newspaper. "Of course. We have so much because we're very, very lucky." She paused portentously. "And if you work very, very hard, the way your father does, you will be lucky, too."

He smiled. Maybe that did sum up a central paradox as far as his mother understood it. But working hard didn't always leave him with an easy conscience. Maybe he'd like to see things evened out a little more. Blake restlessly ran a hand over his hair. His father would think all that sounded pretty communistic, he supposed. He realized his head felt tight and uncomfortable, as if he were about to get a headache. "I think I may turn in early tonight."

"I hope you're not coming down with something."

Blake smiled grimly. "I hope not, too."

NINE

When Susan and Jesse came out of the dinner theater, the moon barely shone through the heavy gray cloud cover. Fog hovered over the wet grass and gutters and made halos around the parking lot lights. Jesse kissed the nape of Susan's neck and hugged her close for a minute. "I hope the highway isn't fogged over."

"We'll just go slow."

"Right."

"It's so pretty, though." Susan whirled around in a little pirouette on the pavement. She felt her foot go cold as it landed unprotected by her flimsy sandal in a puddle. The weather lost its charm as a chill shook her.

"Yuck!" She made a rueful face as she limped to the car. "Don't look," she said when she got in. While Jesse turned away she wiggled out of her sodden panty hose. "Ooo, double yuck," she said. She wadded her panty hose up and stuffed them into her pocketbook. "Okay. That's it. I probably ought to just throw them out. My stockings, I mean. They always run anyway."

"Aren't you still cold? Give me your foot and I'll dry it off." Jesse produced a handkerchief from his jacket and Susan obediently maneuvered her foot up to his knee.

He rubbed her foot dry, blowing off the tiny bits of debris that clung to her toes. "You have very nice feet."

"Thank you."

He stuck out his tongue at her and grinned. "Let's get this heater on." He started the motor but only cold air blew out. "It takes it awhile to warm up."

When Susan had imagined being in love, she had pictured it as romantic dances, flowers, and long, long talks during which no secrets were hidden. It seemed odd to her that what she focused on now were basic, simple things— warmth and roughness of Jesse's hands, the feel of his breath on her cheek. Sometimes all her chatter died away and she only wanted to smell his hair and let his voice sound in her head, not even listening to his words.

Pockets of fog hugged the highway, magnifying headlights into a great blur of light that was frighteningly inadequate. The Camaro slowed to a crawl.

"Jeez, look at that idiot with one of his lights out," said Jesse. "He ought to be locked up."

His attention wasn't on her now. He had to stare fixedly at the road. The heater was pumping warm air on her feet, but she shivered anyway.

Jesse kept leaning forward every couple of minutes to wipe the haze of moisture off the windshield. Sensing his tension, she kept quiet as they crept forward.

Twenty-five miles later, the fog turned to rain. At first it was a drizzle, but then the drops thickened and they were in the middle of a rainstorm. "Unsettled conditions at the edge of the warm front," Jesse commented. "That's what the weatherman said." The rain pounded hard on the metal roof of the car in a continuous low roar. Now and then, lightning illuminated the whole scene.

"My parents are going to be worried if I'm real late," said Susan.

"Sorry. But it'd be worse if they had to claim our bodies at the morgue."

She saw through the haze of rain that some cars pulled off to the shoulder. "Maybe we should pull over." She looked at him anxiously.

"No, I think we ought to keep going. Somebody might hit us if we stop. You can't see all that well. I can barely even make out the center line."

The roar of the blinding rain cut them off from the world. When they went under an overpass, it was blissful to have a brief second free from the noise before they immediately plunged back into the storm.

After a while Jesse said, "It's letting up. I can see pretty well now. I think we're driving out of it."

Susan could hear the faint clicking sound the windshield wipers made, so she knew it was true. The rain was not coming down nearly so hard as it had been. When she rubbed a clear spot on her side of the windshield she could see. By now they had come most of the distance toward home. In fact, she saw that they were coming to the outskirts of town and a traffic light.

Past the traffic light Susan could make out flashing blue lights. The oscillating lights were so disorienting that she couldn't tell how many police cars were at the scene. Maybe two. Or three. Orange fluorescent cones stood in the roadway blocking the right lane. A policeman in a slicker was directing traffic around three cars sitting at odd angles on the road. "Fender bender," said Jesse. "That's all. Probably nobody's hurt."

Soon the red lights of a Zip Mart swam in the runnels of water on Susan's window. She was glad to recognize the turn off from the highway to her neighborhood. She held her watch up close to her eye as they passed the Zip Mart, but the light flickered so briefly she couldn't make out the time.

"We're pretty late." Jesse had noticed her trying to check the time. "But it could have been worse."

With a jolt, Susan remembered that she was supposed to be out with Blake. "Let me off at the corner. I'll walk the rest of the way."

"Do you really think I'm going to let you walk down the block at midnight in the pouring rain?"

Hearing the edge in his voice, she was silent. He was obviously strung out from the long drive in the rain and fog. It was not the time to argue. And she realized that, quite apart from Jesse's state of mind, there were problems. It would look pretty funny if she came in the house dripping wet. Her plan had seemed so simple when she thought it up. It was hard to realize that an incoming warm front had ruined it.

Her pulse quickened in panic. "You could drop me off at the doughnut shop. I could call Blake to come get me. Or if he wouldn't I could get a cab. I could tell my parents that Blake made a pass at me and that I had to call a cab, and—"

"You could shut up, Susan. I'm going to drive you right up to your door. I've had enough."

There was a crashing finality to the way Jesse said "enough" that silenced her. She had never seen him really angry before, and looking at him now, Susan had an anxious, aching feeling in her throat.

It wouldn't be so bad if they hadn't been late, she thought. But her parents would be looking out the window, watching for her. They would see Jesse's car.

He drove the Camaro up the driveway, stopping a couple of yards short of the garage door. The rain turned to crystal in the beams of his headlights. "You want me to go in with you?"

"No. No, I'll just— Do I have my pocketbook?" Flustered, she twisted around in the seat looking for her purse. She bent to pull her sandals off and clutched them to her chest. Then she stuck her leg tentatively outside the open car door, ducked her head, and ran. The wet grass slipped under her bare toes and she squeezed her eyes almost shut against the rain as she ran to the door. She could hear the Camaro's motor idling behind her. Why didn't he drive off? she thought desperately. Her parents might not have spotted him yet!

When she reached the front door and was standing under the portico out of the rain, she glanced and saw Jesse's car still in the driveway. He was waiting to make sure she got in the house okay. As she fumbled with her key the front door flew open. She blinked in the sudden bright light.

"Susan?" Her mother and dad were standing together at the door. Susan heard the Camaro's motor shifting into gear. Jesse was backing out of the driveway. Her parents looked puzzled. They had seen the car, all right. Susan turned and watched the Camaro until it disappeared into the darkness and the rain. For a sickening instant she had the sensation Jesse was driving out of her life.

"What happened?" asked her father. "Was there an accident? Was somebody hurt?"

Susan went inside. She looked ruefully down at the sandals. They were probably ruined. "No, I mean, yes. There was an accident but we weren't in it," she said softly. "We just had to drive really slow because it was all rain and fog between here and Raleigh. You could hardly see a thing. It was awful to drive in."

"But what happened to Blake's car?" Her mother's forehead was creased.

Susan took a shuddering breath. "Oh. I didn't go to Raleigh with Blake, really."

"What are you talking about?"

"Listen, is there some perfectly simple explanation for this? Because I'm not following you at all. What happened?" Her father held up his hand to stop her mother from speaking. "Now, don't say a word. Let's just let Susan tell us what happened. Begin at the beginning."

"The beginning?" Avoiding their eyes, Susan threw herself onto the couch. "We went to the dinner theater in Raleigh like I said, but I didn't go with Blake. Actually, I went with Jesse. Jesse McCracken." She tensed and waited for the explosion.

"McCracken!" Mr. Brantley's face was suddenly suffused with blood. As Susan looked at him fearfully, everything about him seemed to get bigger. "You don't mean to tell me you were out with that trigger-happy redneck's kid! You must be out of your mind!"

"Sit down, dear. Think about your blood pressure."

Mr. Brantley paced the floor. "You tried to think of what would drive me absolutely around the bend and you came up with this, right? You tried to think of what was the worst thing you could do to me. You're trying to give me a heart attack. You're trying to kill me.''

"Why does it always have to do with you?" Susan wailed. "This isn't about you, Daddy. It's about *me*. It's my life!''

"I don't understand, Susan," her mother said. "Why did you lie to us?''

"Ask Dad, he's the one having the heart attack.''

"I'm not going to take that kind of lip from you young lady. When I think how you went running off with this *trash*! You know what kind of people we're talking about here. These people murdered Muffin." Her father choked on a sob. "The law can't touch people like that. They can kill your dog and you just have to sit back and watch them. And now my own daughter is running around with them. My own daughter!''

"Susan, has this been going on long?''

"A while.''

"How long is a while? Have you been seeing this boy every weekend instead of going to the mall?''

Susan nodded. She felt like a human sacrifice. Bitterness rose in her mouth at the thought of Jesse driving off and leaving her to face this.

"Look what it comes to," roared her father. "You give a kid everything—what about that computer we got you for Christmas, missy? What about your car? You just think you don't owe us anything, that's it, isn't it? You kids think you can do anything you please. Well, let me tell you this. As long as you're under my roof you're going to do as I say. Do you hear me? I'm not going to have you sneaking around and going out with trash behind my back, do you hear?''

"Maybe I wouldn't have to sneak around if you would be a little bit reasonable. Do you honestly think you're being reasonable now?'' Susan's voice quavered and she felt her insides contract her in fear. "Because I don't. I think you're being absolutely and totally unfair.''

"Don't you lecture me, young lady!''

"Jason, you'd better let me talk to her. You're getting too wrought up.''

"Wrought up! I should say I'm wrought up!'' Mr. Brantley screamed. "You want to see angry? You've got angry! This puts the cork on it. When I think I can't trust my own flesh and blood!''

"Just go, Jason.'' Mrs. Brantley put her hands on her husband's shoulders and gave him a gentle push out of the room. "Let me talk to her.''

"Don't think you've heard the last of this, Susan. Do you hear me?''

After her father left, the room seemed quiet. Susan sighed. "I want to go to bed, Mom. I'm really tired. I don't need all this.''

Her mother sat down beside her. "Susan, you may not think I understand this, but I do. I went through my own rebellion. Something that's forbidden may seem attractive. But that doesn't mean it's good for us, does it? Don't you honestly feel ashamed of yourself?''

Susan shook her head, tears stinging her eyes. "I haven't been doing anything wrong! Jesse is a terrific person. You won't even give him a chance. Why do you have to keep on me like I'm some kind of criminal? It's so unfair! I haven't done anything wrong, you hear?''

"You call lying and sneaking doing nothing wrong?''

"But I wouldn't have to do that if it weren't for Dad. You heard him. He's like a crazy person.''

"He is naturally very upset. I think you might have a little consideration for your father's feelings.''

"What about my feelings? Or is Daddy the only one allowed to have feelings around here?"

"Now, listen to me, Susan. No, don't say a word. Your father was devoted to Muffin and you're reopening all those wounds. It's not fair to him. Now, I don't want to belabor this point. We're all tired. I just want you to give me your solemn promise that you aren't going to see the McCracken boy again."

Susan got up. "I won't promise that."

"Susan!"

"I love him!" She ran upstairs.

Susan threw herself on her bed, hot tears burning her eyes. For a second she felt as if she were choking. Her whole body shook with sobs. She had half expected her mother to come after her, but she didn't. After a while Susan blew her nose, stripped off her clothes, pulled on a flannel nightgown, and got into bed shivering. She felt sick and alone. She kept thinking about Jesse's car driving off into the darkness. It was easy for him. He didn't have to have people scream at him.

The next morning Susan crept down to breakfast, her stomach still upset over what had happened the night before. Her mother was in the kitchen dressed in her flowered bathrobe. Her face was calm and she was spreading jam on an English muffin. "What exactly are your plans for today?"

"I don't know."

"You understand that we can't just take your unsupported word for where you're going anymore."

Susan flushed. "I'm not going to lie anymore. Now that you know about Jesse, I don't have anything to hide. I only did all that stuff because Daddy is so weird about Jesse's family."

"I'd like to see you take responsibility for your own actions, for a change, Susan."

Susan was so angry she completely lost her appetite, but she went through the charade of taking a muffin out of the freezer and putting it on a paper towel in the microwave. Not that she'd eat it. Her mouth felt like cotton.

"Tell me about this boy."

Susan turned to face her. "Mom, he's wonderful. He's really responsible, and nice, and hard-working. He's a pitcher for the baseball team and he's good. He may be able to turn pro, even."

"What kind of boy sneaks around to see a girl behind her parents' back?"

"If you're going to be that way, there's no sense in talking about it."

"Don't think I'm not sympathetic to your problem, Susan."

"You don't sound very sympathetic. Jesse was *against* us sneaking around. He was always on me about it."

"I have to think about your father's health. We can't have this boy coming to the house and have your father carried off in a fit at the sight of him."

"Well, whose fault would that be? You can't stop me from seeing Jesse, Mom. If you take my car away, I'll walk. Take away my computer, if you want. Take my allowance. I'll get a part-time job."

"That will be some trick without a car."

"There are buses."

"Susan, be reasonable. Try to look at this from our point of view for a minute."

"No, thanks."

"I'm not going to say any more about this now," her mother said softly. "I just want you to think about it."

Susan had already thought about it. That was what had kept her up so late the night before. That was why her head ached this morning. She had thought it out very carefully, and it was all perfectly clear. She was at war with her family.

Her eye fell on the calendar. "Oh, my *gosh!*" she moaned. "I've got to go. Now. This is the day of the bake sale!"

TEN

When Susan arrived at the home ec kitchen, it was warm and smelled of yeast and chocolate. Kids were pounding on mounds of dough every place and the noise level was high.

"Susan," cried Mrs. Armstrong. "We'd just about given up on you."

"My alarm didn't go off," she mumbled.

Jesse stood near the refrigerator stirring nuts into chocolate batter. He looked up at the sound of Susan's voice. She edged her way past a bunch of kids until she reached him.

"How'd it go?"

She grimaced.

"I should have gone in with you."

"No, I don't think that would have been good, actually."

"Well, what did they say?"

"Just about what you'd expect. They screamed and yelled and told me I couldn't see you anymore." She swallowed.

"So what happens now?"

"I don't know. They can't stop me from going out with you. It's against the law to chain your daughter in her room."

"That's not very funny."

"I'm not laughing."

"You think telling them was a mistake, don't you?"

Susan shook her head. She took the bowl from him and began to stir the brownie mixture. "I think it was more or less inevitable, to tell you the truth. I thought about it all night. Like you said, sooner or later they were bound to find out." Susan could feel a passivity fall over her that was almost like peace. She supposed she was becoming a fatalist.

Mrs. Armstrong's voice pealed out. "As soon as we get that bread set aside to rise, we can start on the cookies. Let's get a move on. Hurry, hurry, people."

"We're still kneading," Tucker protested. "We're not anywhere near ready."

Mrs. Armstrong bent over the bread dough Rainey and Tucker had been pummeling and examined it critically. "It's supposed to be shiny. I guess you'd better keep at it. But we've got to get it done in time to catch the lunch crowds at the mall. It's no use trying to sell food to people when they've just eaten."

After Mrs. Armstrong moved away, Tucker said, "You know what you ought to do, Rainey? You ought to send your story in to one of those magazines. Maybe *Tales of Terror*, or *Horror Ninjas and Mutants*."

"I've already thought of that. I'm sending it off as soon as I get it typed up."

"I bet they'll buy it. Heck, it's better than most of the stuff you see in those magazines."

The trouble was, Rainey thought, it might take weeks to hear from the magazine. Months, even. She had no idea how long it took or how much those magazines paid, but she was afraid the answers were "too long" and "not enough." She was worried about her father sleeping in that gold, damp tobacco barn. What if he got pneumonia? and lately she'd been brooding a lot about what would happen if he got caught. He'd probably be sent off to prison where horrible things happened to people. She hastily wiped away a tear. A smudge of dough smeared on her cheek.

"Hold still." Tucker dabbed at her cheek with a towel.

She managed a semblance of a smile. "This dough is tough on the arms. Do you think it's looking shiny yet?"

Tucker considered the ball of dough. "I don't know. It's just wet flour, isn't it? How could it look shiny? Maybe it's never going to get shiny. Maybe this is Mrs. A's idea of a sick joke, the whole class pounding on dough until they pass out."

Blake was at the long table in the center of the kitchen making cinnamon buns with Michael and Ann Lee. He had made peanut butter cookies once in grade school and it had been a cinch. Who would have figured that making cinnamon buns was only slightly less complicated than constructing the Parthenon?

"We must have done something wrong," he protested. "This junk isn't suppose to stick to the table. I don't see how we can roll the dough up if it sticks to the table."

"Maybe we could just scoop it all up in a pile," Michael suggested. "We could call it cinnamon cake."

"Mrs. Armstrong!" bleated Ann Lee.

"It looks like an industrial accident, " said Michael.

Mrs. Armstrong came over to their table. "Oh, dear!" She prodded the dough. It stuck to her finger. "Oh, dear, oh, dear."

Glancing over at the counter at the end of the room, Blake noticed that Tucker and Rainey had at last stopped kneading and were draping a dish towel over a bowl. Those two had been inseparable all morning. It had even crossed Blake's mind that their pairing off might be just another of Rainey's ploys to avoid him. The hundred-dollar bill burned in his hip pocket. He needed to get Rainey alone, but he didn't see how he could do it. The kitchen was unbelievably crowded. Maybe it would be easier once they finished with the baking and went to the mall.

"Maybe if we just added a little flour to this," Mrs. Armstrong said. "Are you sure you measured all the ingredients carefully?"

Blake thought the dough was beginning to look like Jabba the Hut the day after meltdown.

"Throw on another handful of flour," Mrs. Armstrong panted. Ann Lee spattered flour onto the table. Half of it landed on Mrs. Armstrong. Her forearms were white. Even her hair was dusted with it.

Blake and Michael leaned against the kitchen cabinets and tried to pretend they had nothing to do with the cinnamon bun disaster. Michael spoke almost without moving his lips. "Cynthia heard from Richmond yesterday."

"Yeah?"

"She's taking the job."

"I guess you're happy for her. More or less."

"I may kill myself."

"Maybe the cinnamon buns will explode and save you the trouble."

"What do you think about the idea of me going up to Richmond with her?"

"Heck, it doesn't matter what I think. The question is what does she think? Are you serious about this?"

"I don't know. Sounds kind of like a crazy idea, doesn't it?"

Blake shrugged.

"What's the matter with you, man? You're supposed to be telling me what an awful idea it is. You ought to threaten to tie me up and save me from myself and all that good stuff. What's happened to the old fire? The stern disapproval? Jeez, I may have to get myself another friend."

"Yeah."

"Oh, come on, I was just kidding. What's the matter with you, anyway?"

"Nothing."

"Look, I'm the one who's supposed to be depressed around here. Who do you think you are?"

"Oh, come on. Lay off. You aren't the only one in the world with troubles, you know."

"Oh, yeah? What kind of troubles have you got, Blake old buddy. Go ahead. Tell me. Leaf mold on your car? B-plus on an English test? Pour it all out, pal. I'm not the kind to dump on a friend who's bleeding all over the place, unlike some people I could name."

"Cut it out, would you?" Blake suspected the smell of cinnamon would forever be associated in his mind with unhappiness. He watched Tucker put his hand on Rainey's waist. She was giggling. Even though so many girls had fallen for Tucker, Blake was surprised to see it happening to Rainey. He had expected her to notice how superficial and slick Tucker was. After all, she wasn't like those girls around the swimming pool.

"Tucker, Rainey!" yodeled Mrs. Armstrong. "If you've finished the kneading, you can get started on the cookies now."

"Maybe we should get started doing cookies, too, Mrs. Armstrong," Michael said. "These cinnamon rolls really need a special touch, a certain expertise, a certain finesse that I must humbly confess is beyond me. Maybe we ought to pitch what we've got into the trash and make, uh—"

"Peanut butter cookies," supplied Blake.

The two friends smiled uneasily at each other.

"No, no. I think we can salvage this, boys. Now don't get discouraged. We're getting there. Try to find me some waxed paper, okay?"

"Where are the cooling racks?" screeched Marilyn Hastings. "My cookies are ready to come out."

Cookie sheets rattled and the pace in the kitchen quickened perceptibly as kids began pushing batches and batches of cookies in and out of the kitchen's three ovens.

"Mine look kind of burned around the edges," Tom Kelly said.

Mrs. Armstrong glanced at his cookie sheet. "They're just nicely browned."

"We ought to taste them." Michael suggested. "Just to make sure they're all right."

"Touch one and you're dead, Michael," said Mrs. Armstrong.

"Okay by me," muttered Michael.

Mrs. Armstrong washed her hands and dabbed ineffectually at her hair. "Is that better? How do I look?"

"Like the ghost of Hamlet's father," said Michael.

"Maybe I'd better go brush out my hair."

While Mrs. Armstrong retired to the ladies' room, the kids stuck to their tasks. At length the various batches of bread had risen and were in the ovens. Meanwhile the number of cookies on the worktable had reached alarming proportions. Cookies were laid out on cooling racks, mounded up in bowls, and piled in heaps on the counter.

Mrs. Armstrong lined up a bunch of kids at the long table and set them to work putting the cookies into small plastic bags. Two boys at the end of the table were assigned the job of sticking price tags on the plastic bags.

"But gently," cried Mrs. Armstrong. "Don't break the cookies."

Tucker and Rainey pulled their loaf out of the oven, looked at each other and beamed with pride.

"Beautiful!" Tucker smiled. "Our first joint production, and a very classy product, if I do say so myself."

Rainey liked the way Tucker was already speaking of the two of them as a couple. She felt as if she were hanging on tight to an island of security while the worries about her father wheeled treacherously around her.

The bread smelled even better than the cookies or the brownies and once the loaves began coming out of the ovens, a feeling of achievement began to percolate through the class. Kids were smiling and joking as they packed the baked goods into the van.

Blake punched Michael lightly on the arm. "Look, I didn't mean to dump on you. I guess I'm in a pretty foul mood."

"I noticed. Hey, that's okay, man. My understanding nature is famous. Besides, I'm going to need every friend I've got once Cynthia's gone." The corners of Michael's mouth were turned down.

When the class got to the mall, they set up card tables near the fountain. Sheets of poster board fastened to the tables with masking tape proclaimed "Bake Sale. West Mount High."

A few yards away, Girl Scouts in uniform were selling cookies from card tables. Their poster board was decorated with green trefoils and the legend "Girl Scout Cookies."

"Will you look at that?" Mrs. Armstrong glared at the rosy-cheeked girls. "The mall management didn't tell me we'd be competing against the Scouts."

"Want me to hire a hit man?" asked Michael.

"Sure," said Blake. "Let's rub out the Girl Scouts. Great public-relations idea."

"I was only trying to help."

"Listen, people," said Mrs. Armstrong. "There's no need for all of us to sit at the card tables. We can work in shifts. Let's have six people at the card tables and the rest of you can go to lunch. Just be sure to report back here to find out what time you're supposed to help cover the tables."

"I'm ready for lunch," said Susan.

Jesse suddenly went rigid. "Good grief, Susan, isn't that your mom?"

Mrs. Brantley had just come in the mall's main entrance. She hesitated there a moment, an attractive blond woman in sensible shoes and a brown suede coat. Her eyes scanned the group of kids who were rapidly fanning out all over the mall.

"Mom!" Susan raised her arms and waved.

"I'm out of here," said Jesse.

"No." Susan grabbed his arm. "You stay."

Mrs. Brantley strode over to them. "I thought I might catch you here."

Susan's grip on Jesse's arm tightened. 'Mom, this is Jesse."

Her mother smiled. "I thought I might find you here, too, Jesse. Why don't we all have lunch? Do you like pizza?"

"The pizza here is terrible," Susan said.

"Well, but we don't care about the food, do we? We just want to get to know each other better."

Susan and Jesse exchanged a glance and Susan shrugged.

Blake watched Jesse and Susan and Mrs. Brantley walk away in the direction of the café plaza and wondered idly what was going on. He was sitting on the bricks that ran around the fountain, his hands in his pockets. He had about decided that the only way he was ever going to catch Rainey alone was to wait until Tucker had to go to the men's room. Then he glanced toward the entrance and spotted Rainey there. She appeared to be at loose ends. He jumped up.

The color drained from her face when she saw him, but she didn't run away. Blake grabbed her arms.

"Rainey, look. You don't have to tell me anything, but just stay here a minute. I've got something to give you."

"To give me?"

He pulled out the hundred-dollar bill. Rainey looked at it in bewilderment.

"It's a loan," he said quickly. "You can pay it back whenever you can."

She gulped and took a step back. He knows, she thought.

"Don't be stupid about this, Rainey. Take it."

"How—how do you know—"

Blake licked his lips. "I don't know anything. I just want to give you this and you can give it back to me later, okay?"

Rainey stared at the hundred-dollar bill, fascinated. That hundred dollars would mean she could drop her dad off at the bus station tomorrow. This afternoon even. She had saved a hundred dollars already and this would bring her up to her goal. But she couldn't bring herself to reach for it.

"Come on, Rainey. People are going to see us." Just then Blake saw Tucker backing in the mall door carrying a tray full of plastic-bagged cookies and bread loaves. Feeling himself grow hot all over, he stuffed the bill into Rainey's jeans pocket, then turned abruptly and walked away.

As Blake walked away, Rainey put her hand in her pocket. Feeling the crisp bill gave her a queasy feeling. It seemed all wrong to take the money. Of course, she would pay Blake back. But, all the same, taking the money made her feel small and young. It made her feel as if she were too weak to handle things on her own.

"What was Blake up to?"

Rainey jumped. "Nothing." The tray Tucker was holding was heaped high with baked goods. "Do you need help with that?" she asked.

"No, I don't need help with that," he snapped. "I've got it this far, haven't I? Rainey, you don't have anything going with Blake, do you?"

"N-no. Why do you ask that?"

"Just checking."

"Hey, Tucker, what are you waiting for?" someone yelled. "Christmas?"

"I've got to go. I've got to get this stuff over there."

Rainey nodded. "I guess it's really selling fast."

Rainey looked around desperately. She needed a way to leave the mall. Now that she had the money, she felt it was tempting fate to hang around one minute longer than necessary. The sense of urgency that boiled within her was almost like panic. Any minute her father could be discovered and here she was hanging around the mall when she actually had all the money she needed. She spotted Michael standing under a neon pretzel sign. It wasn't easy to miss him because

he was big and he was the only kid in their class with graying
hair. She ran over to him.

"Michael," she said breathlessly. "Could you give me
a ride home? Now?"

"What's the matter? Your car on the blink?"

"No, I got a ride with somebody, but now I need to get
home—right away."

"Sure, but I haven't even had lunch yet."

"What's that in your hand?"

He looked down at the giant pretzel. "This is the appe-
tizer. I'm getting warmed up for the main course."

"You'll be back in twenty minutes and then you can eat
your head off. Won't you just run me home now?"

"What's the big rush?"

"I need to get away before Tucker notices. I mean, I
came with him, but now I need to get home. And I . . . "
Her voice trailed off.

"Ah, this is an affair of the heart."

"Sort of. I guess."

"I don't quite follow you, though. What's this with you
and Tucker?"

"Do I have to go into that now?"

Michael sighed. "I understand. You don't want to talk
about it. Oh, believe me, I understand."

"Sure. Heck, if I can do anything to bring a little happiness into the life of a fellow mortal in this miserable vale
of tears, I'm only too happy to oblige." He took a bite of
pretzel. "I mean, you know what they say—life's a bummer
and then you die."

"I'm in sort of a hurry, Michael."

"No problem. I'm coming. Hang on."

Ann Lee came up. She was staring at the menu board in

a state of intense concentration that could have passed for a daze.

"Don't get the hot pretzel," Michael advised her. "They microwave them. Rubbery—bleh!"

Rainey grabbed Michael's hand. "Ann Lee, would you tell Tucker that I had to go home unexpectedly? Something came up."

Ann Lee blinked. "Sure, Rainey."

With no further explanation, Rainey pulled Michael out to his car and got him to drive her home.

Twenty minutes later, when Michael returned to the mall, he ran into Blake.

"Where'd you go, man? I've been looking all over for you.

"Rainey needed a ride home."

Blake felt a twinge of satisfaction that Rainey had not, at least, asked Tucker to take her home. He wondered what excuse she had given Tucker. He hoped it was something flimsy and transparent.

"You didn't get lunch without me, did you?" asked Michael.

"Nah. I started to go to the pizza place but Susan and Jesse and her mom were in there having a heart-to-heart so I got out of there.

After considering all twelve restaurants, Michael and Blake settled on the Submarine Solarium. There, surrounded by tropical plants, which looked as if they were made of plastic, Michael expanded on the theme of how empty his life would be once Cynthia had left.

"She's already handed in her notice," he said.

"That's good."

"Look, man, are you listening to anything I've been saying?"

"Sure. Sure, I'm listening. Mostly. Hey, Michael, you remember a long time ago you asked me if I ever wanted something?"

"It rings a small bell."

"Well, I do."

"Okay, I'll bite. What do you want?"

"I'm not ready to talk about it."

"Great, this is great. I'm pouring my heart out all over the table and you talk in acrostics. What is it? Something about your car?"

"No. I'm not talking about a car."

Michael covered his eyes and groaned. "You know, Blake, this is why I need a woman. This is one of the reasons why anyway. I don't want you to take this personally or anything, but you are just about the worst listener in the history of the world. And to top it off, you've got all the charming openness of a mollusk. What do you think I'm going to do? Take out a half-page ad in the paper to broadcast your secret? I mean, give me a break. You are insulting your best friend, you hear me?"

"It's Rainey."

"What's Rainey?"

"Rainey is what I want."

Michael looked at him blankly for a minute. "Oh, well, what's the problem? Have you told her?"

"I think she knows."

"You can't expect girls to read your mind, you know. You've got to go after them. Like I *pursued* Cynthia, you know? That's the way it's done. They're flattered that you care enough to make an idiot out of yourself, I guess." Michael suddenly looked glum.

"There may be problems."

"Like what?"

Blake remembered the look on Rainey's face when he had given her the hundred-dollar bill. He had only meant to help, but she had looked at him as if he'd hit her. "I can't tell you."

"Okay, that's enough. Miss? Miss, would you like to sit here? This guy used to be my best friend, but lately he's gotten kind of weird. I think a persuasive case could be put for the theory that an android has been substituted for a seemingly innocuous high-school student. He looks the same, you see, talks the same, but if you look just below his left eyebrow—"

The young woman hastily moved to a distant booth, glancing over her shoulder as she fled.

"Will you cut it out, Michael? People are going to think we're nuts."

"So what?"

"Let's get out of here. This is embarrassing."

Michael shrugged, but got up. They walked back toward the fountain eating their sandwiches.

"Well, it's no big deal, really," Blake said finally. "It's just that I was able to help Rainey out about something and I don't think she liked it."

"Real independent, Rainey."

"Yeah."

"Kind of on the bossy side, too."

"Nah."

"Rainey, huh?"

"Would you stop acting like I'm out of my mind?"

"I didn't say that. I might have *thought* it, but I didn't say it. No, I mean, Rainey's a good kid. You just do the best you can do, pal. Go after her. That's all you can do."

"Yeah. I know."

"Michael, Blake, get over here!" Mrs. Armstrong waved

at them. "We need people to cover these tables. The entire class had vanished. I feel as if I've dropped a school of guppies into the ocean. Where has everybody gone?"

Ann Lee and a few other obedient types were busy selling cookies and bread, but it was evident they could use some help. Michael and Blake moved in behind one of the card tables and Michael started counting out change for Ann Lee.

A middle-aged man picked up a plastic bag and looked at it suspiciously. "What's this?"

Michael glanced at it. "Oh, that, sir. That's a cinnamon spike. Notice how hard and sharp-edged it is. It's the weapon of the twenty-first century. No waste, no radioactive fallout. And we're offering it today at a very special price."

The man dropped the plastic bag in alarm.

"Shut up, Michael," Ann Lee said. "We've got some nice brownies, sir."

Michael turned the cinnamon bun over in his big hands, examining it critically. "I don't know. I think we may be on to something here. Has anybody been in touch with the Pentagon?"

"The bread is selling very well." Mrs. Armstrong gave Blake her keys. "Will you go out to the van and get another trayful?"

Blake clambered out from behind the tables. The more he thought about the business with Rainey, the more uncomfortable he felt. He wondered where she was now. Presumably, if he had the situation sized up properly, she was trying to get her dad out of town as quickly as possible. He just hoped she didn't get caught doing it. He wondered if she realized that the police had taken to searching luggage on buses in their effort to cut the drug traffic. He wished he had actually gone over the details with her. Maybe he could have made some helpful suggestions. He could even have driven her father to the station. Since nobody would connect him with the fugitive, it would have been safe enough. He stopped himself short. What was he thinking about? Did he want to end up in jail? It was a good thing he didn't know about it officially. It would be even better if Rainey didn't. He would be glad to see her safe and sound back at the mall. He supposed there wasn't any chance she was planning to leave with her father. That wouldn't make any sense, would it?

Blake was so preoccupied that he collided with a bunch of kids.

"Watch where you're going, Farraby!" snapped Tucker. "You bumped up against me."

Blake had had enough of Tucker. "I'll bump up against you any time I want."

The kids around Tucker backed away hastily.

"You will, huh?" Tucker grabbed Blake's shoulder. Blake threw off his hand with an impatient shrug.

"You think you're pretty hot, don't you!" Tucker drew back a fist, but Blake landed his punch first. The thud of his fist on the bone of Tucker's face was strangely satisfying.

"Fight!" a shrill voice shrieked. Blake and Tucker were not the kind of guys who generally ended up in fights, and the kids watching looked on in wide-eyed astonishment.

A cut opened over Tucker's eye and the blood obscured his vision slightly as he struck out at Blake.

"Oomph," Tucker grunted. He backed away, then suddenly straightened and his fist flew out, grazing Blake's chin.

Blake felt his teeth jar and the shooting pain of the blow. In a rage, he struck out again and this time Tucker landed on the floor. Blake looked down at him and smiled.

"Hey! Mall security!" someone yelled.

Blake swore. Tucker scrambled up and they both looked around hastily. A couple of uniformed figures could be seen hustling in their direction.

Blake ran for the entrance and as soon as he was outside looked around frantically. Unfortunately his car was parked on the other side of the lot. He forced himself to breathe deeply and walk slowly along the sidewalk. He reasoned that if he were not running, the security men would have a hard time distinguishing him from the other figures straggling through the parking lot. After a couple of minutes of that, his nerve cracked. He ducked into the first door he came to, which turned out to be that of a discount store. He took out his handkerchief and blotted the blood off his chin. He stood for a while, collecting himself and pretending to be engrossed in a sale on sweatshirts. He flushed a little when it dawned on him he was looking at a sweatshirt emblazoned with a large image of Tweety Bird.

He couldn't believe he had actually hit Tucker. Now that the first rush of anger was over, he felt slightly sick to his stomach. He only hoped he hadn't done any actual damage to the creep. He hated to think of ending up in court with his father having to hire some high-powered Raleigh lawyer to defend him. He would never live it down. And how would it look on his transcript? He couldn't figure out if this would be the same as a fight on school grounds or not. After all, the bake sale was a kind of school event. Suddenly Blake felt the extra pair of keys in his pocket. "Jeez," he said out loud. He had forgotten that he had Mrs. Armstrong's keys.

Glancing around quickly, he went over to the discount store's service desk. A bored young woman was reading a magazine there. "Uh, is it possible to have somebody paged in the mall?" Blake asked.

"Not really. We can page them in the store, but you can't

really hear that out on the mall, you know?'' The girl went back to her magazine.

''Well, maybe I guess I'd better try to have him paged in the store.'' If he was lucky, he figured, Michael might hear and he wouldn't have to go out into the mall to return Mrs. Armstong's keys.

The girl picked up a microphone and said, ''Michael Dessaseaux. Would Michael Dessaseaux please come to the service desk? Michael Dessaseaux.'' She flipped over the page of the magazine.

''Thank you.'' Blake smiled weakly.

''Sure.''

''I'll just, uh, hang around here, I guess.''

The girl didn't look up.

Blake studied trolleys full of women's blouses in large sizes for seven dollars. They featured fluorescent-looking pink and blue flower designs that might have given a sensitive person nightmares. He stood there, wondering what he was going to do, when suddenly Michael appeared.

''Man, what got into you?''

''Not so loud.'' Blake looked around him guiltily. ''I've got to give you the keys to Mrs. Armstrong's van.''

''Cindy Dixon told me they were paging me in here and I put two and two together. Look, cool out. It's okay. We've sold out of bread but the brownies are still going strong and we've still got all of the cinnamon spikes.'' Michael put the keys in his pocket.

''What happened?'' Blake asked. ''Did they get Tucker?''

''Nah, he ducked into an antique store and got this sudden deep interest in a cherry bureau. For all I know, he had to buy the sucker. What'd he do to you?''

"Nothing. I don't know what got into me. I've never done anything like that before."

"Blake, Blake, Blake."

"Aren't things bad enough without you sobbing all over these stinking blouses?"

"You gotta get a grip, man. Life ain't easy."

"I've noticed. Okay, look, just give those keys to Mrs. Armstrong."

"We ought to look on the bright side. You got away clean and nobody's talking. These may be degenerate times, but I'm happy to say that the code of West Mount holds fast. Everybody's saying that it all happened so fast they couldn't really see anything. But they think it was kids from some other school."

Blake sagged a little. "That's great. Well, look, I'm out of here."

He had the awful feeling that he was messing things up from start to finish. He couldn't believe he had socked Tucker. Tucker was half a head shorter than he was. How did it look? He didn't even like to think about it. Rainey would probably never want to see him again after this, and almost as bad, he had let Tucker know how much he could get to him. The sleaze ball was probably congratulating himself right now. Blake figured what he needed to do was go home and hide out in bed so he couldn't do anything else wrong. Michael was right. He needed to get a grip on himself.

ELEVEN

*R*ainey got the ticket from the clerk at the bus station and took it out to the car. Her father was in the front seat wearing dark glasses and a hat. As she approached the car, she tried to look at him as if he were a stranger. He didn't, she decided, look any more peculiar than the other people in the bus station.

She got in the car and gave him the ticket. "It leaves in ten minutes and I don't see any cops. I think we're okay."

"Why would there be any cops? I didn't expect them. Things mostly work out, don't they, hon?"

"I guess." Actually, she disagreed. Things didn't mostly work out. But she didn't want to get into an argument with her father. A strange tenderness and sadness swept over her whenever she was with him. Just thinking about him, she could get angry with him, but face to face she couldn't.

"Sometimes I wonder if I've lived my life all wrong," he said. "You know? But what are you going to do? I don't want to get to the end of the road and say, well, I spent my life selling used cars, never did a thing to change the system, just went along pretending everything was okay."

Rainey wasn't sure whether her father had lived his life all wrong or not. Maybe he had. But she hated for him to be sad about it. She wished he were like the men in the Junior Chamber of Commerce—plump and prosperous. She had seen their pictures in the paper—men like Susan's father with self-important smiles. It seemed awful to her that her father had to sleep in a cold tobacco barn and saddest of all that he had to come to her for help.

A fat woman with two bulging suitcases was going in the bus station door.

"I'm going in, now, I guess," he said.

"Don't you think you'd better wait a little longer?"

"Nope, I don't want to get everybody's attention by hurrying. Haven't you noticed that nobody ever hurries in a bus station?"

"Okay. Whatever you think."

"Bye-bye, sweetheart. Your pappa's going to be out of your hair now."

"You take care of yourself. Do you have those vitamins I gave you?"

"Sure thing." He grinned and in the network of lines on his face she saw the shadow of the handsome young man her mother had married.

Impulsively she reached over and hugged him. "Bye, Pappa."

She watched as he walked into the station, her face wet

with tears. She quickly wiped a sleeve across her face. She knew she had to wait in the car, just in case he needed help at the last minute. But after a while she saw the bus pull out. Light glanced off its big windows making it look blank and sightless. Its brakes sighed.

It doesn't matter, she told herself as she watched the bus drive away down Main Street. I'm not the same as my father. I'm not the same as my mother. I'm me, wonderful me. For me everything is going to be all right. I have enough initiative to make it turn out all right. Trying hard to ignore the lump in her throat, she drove home.

When she walked in the phone was ringing. To her ears it sounded as if it had been ringing a long time. She picked up the receiver. "Hello?"

"Rainey? Why'd you run off like that?"

It was Tucker.

"I remembered something I had to do at home." That was true enough, anyway.

"What?"

"You aren't going to be one of those boys that counts every breath a girl takes, are you?"

"This didn't have anything to do with Blake, did it?"

Rainey swallowed. She was thinking guiltily of the money Blake had given her. "Why do you say that?"

"You sound funny, Rainey."

"We've been having trouble with the connection." She jiggled the phone a few times to lend believability to her claim.

"Well, the reason I ask is the creep hauled off and socked me."

"Blake? You mean Blake hauled off and socked you?"

"You don't believe me? You want to come see my black

eye? I'm sitting here by the phone with a cold steak on it. I'm serious.''

"I was just surprised, that's all. I've never ever heard of Blake getting into a fight.''

"You didn't tell him anything about me, did you?''

"Good grief, no. That's a pretty weird question. What would I tell him?''

"I just don't want to get caught up in one of these sticky triangle things. One time—well, never mind. I guess he's just jealous.''

"You sound pretty happy for a guy who's just been socked.''

"Well, it all evens out. Blake's got the fast right arm and I've got you.''

"What did you say?''

"Want to go to a movie tonight?''

Rainey's heart lightened thinking about life as a normal person, as signified by going to a movie on a Saturday night. All the fringe worries—about her father getting to New York safely and about owing Blake a hundred dollars— faded a little around the edges. "Sure.'' She smiled. "I'd love to.''

Back at the mall Susan, Jesse, and Mrs. Brantley were sitting in a booth at the pizza parlor. A couple of cold pizza slices lay on the stainless steel plate before them and some peppermint rounds weighed down the check at the side of the table.

"After my grandfather died, the farm was split up between my father's brothers and sisters, and no one piece of it was really big enough to be a paying farm. It's practically impossible to make a small farm pay, anyway, these days. So my dad works at the diesel engine plant—he's a plant supervisor—

and he just does a little farming on the side. We've got chickens and ducks, and we're raising some calves. One year we grew seed tobacco. It's more like a hobby, actually.''

Susan was finding out things about Jesse that she didn't even know, things they had never gotten around to talking about. It was a strange sensation. But when she tried to step away emotionally and see him through her mother's eyes, she couldn't. She was too close to him to see him as a stranger would.

"So you're not interested in farming, yourself," Mrs. Brantley said.

"Not really. I don't know what I want to do if the baseball doesn't work out. I know it's a long shot, but everything kind of depends on how my pitching goes. I'm going to go ahead and apply to East Carolina, but if I get an offer to go with a farm team somewhere, that's what I'll do.''

"He's really talented, Mom. He's a terrific pitcher."

Jesse flushed. "I'm not bad.''

"Peppermints, anyone?" asked Mrs. Brantley. She picked up the check. "Well, I've enjoyed getting to know you a little better, Jesse."

"Does this mean I can pick up Susan at her house, now?"

Mrs. Brantley hesitated. "Well, maybe we'd better count on a two-week cooling-off period and then if you could just pull up outside, but not actually come in the house, at least at first.''

Susan looked at her mother anxiously but she saw no signs that her mother had any hidden motive and she felt reassured.

"Oh, Susan. I almost forgot. This came for you this morning.''

Her mother groped in her purse and produced an envelope. "It's that summer abroad thing. You got it! Isn't that nice?"

"A summer is a long time—" Ann Lee's words echoed in Susan's head. She looked at the letter with incomprehension. It seemed different to her now that it had seemed when she applied. "We'd better get back to that bake sale," she said. "It's going to look to Mrs. Armstrong as if we ran out on her."

"What about the letter? Well, aren't you excited about it at all?" asked her mother.

"I don't know, Mom. I'm not sure I want to do that anymore." She glanced at Jesse. "In fact, I'm sure I don't."

"I'd thought you'd be thrilled. Mary Smith called me just before I came over here. Ann Lee is first alternate. Mary dreads breaking it to her. She had her heart set on it."

Susan grabbed Jesse's hand and jumped up. "Well, when I drop out, Ann Lee will get to go, right?"

Mrs. Brantley's eyes searched Susan's face. She picked up her purse. "Think it over, Susan. Don't do anything you're going to regret later. We can talk about it after you get home. Nice meeting you, Jesse."

When they left the restaurant, Susan felt such a sense of relief she could have burst into song.

"Don't think you have to pass up that summer thing for me," Jesse said. "If you want to go, do it."

"I don't want to do it. I don't want to go running off to some foreign country when everything I want is right here." A little girl was throwing a coin into the fountain. Susan remembered getting soaked trying to fish dimes out of that fountain when she was little and she smiled. "Besides, I'm not sure I can do without hamburgers and fries for that long."

"Well, like your mother said, think it over."

"Maybe I ought to send you and Mom. You're the ones who think it's such a hot idea."

"I didn't say that. I just don't want your Mom to think I'm cutting you off from some great opportunity." He squeezed her hand. "It seemed to go okay, didn't it? The thing with your mom, I mean."

"She likes you. I can tell. Anybody would like you."

"Why does everything have to be such a hassle? All this drama and stuff when all we want to do is just be together."

"Some things are simple. Like you and me."

"Nothing's simple."

Susan thought about the lunch they had just had. It had been a relief to have her mother talking in a more civilized way to Jesse, and yet in another way it had been difficult and tense. She didn't like to have to take her mother's and father's opinions into account. She didn't like to deal with their anxieties and their craziness. She didn't like having to appreciate her mother's efforts at reconciliation. Why should all that junk be allowed to color her happiness? But the only alternative was sneaking around uneasily, which Jesse had hated. That, she supposed, was life. Maybe Jesse was right. Nothing was ever simple. "This takes care of the problem of the prom, anyway, doesn't it?" she said lightly.

"The prom and other great issues of our time."

"Okay, make fun of me. You were talking about it yourself a while ago."

He pinched her.

"Stop that!"

"Make me." He trotted a few steps ahead of her.

Susan caught up with him and they grabbed hands and whirled around in a circle.

It's going to be all right, Susan thought. Daddy will make

nasty scenes, but he'll fall in line. As she whirled around and around, she could feel her tension turning into laughter. It was going to be all right, she thought. It was going to be all right, after all.

Rainey was washing out a cotton sweater in the sink. It was a soothing activity that kept her from thinking about her father speeding away on a bus going north on I-95. It also kept her from puzzling over Blake, who had somehow mysteriously gone berserk after giving her a hundred dollars. She rinsed the sweater well and laid it out to dry on a towel in the only really open place in the trailer, the space in front of the couch in the living room. Washing clothes by hand was a familiar ritual to Rainey. She took the family clothes to the Laundromat once a week, but she didn't like to put her delicate things in the big washers. Next she dropped a handful of underwear into the sink. After swooshing it about awhile in soapy water, she began to feel there was at least minimal order and reason in her life. The rest of the world might be crazy, but she could count on clean underwear. She had that, anyway. She rinsed it very carefully, blotted it on a towel, tossed it into a basket, and took it outside. Some dandelions were in bloom by the clothesline, and Rainey could feel the sun on her shoulders when she hung up the clothes. Spring was coming.

A banging sound startled her. The front door of the trailer was rattling. The dogs in the trailer park started yipping. Uneasily, Rainey peered around the corner of the trailer, half expecting to see the police hammering on the door. "Blake!" she cried.

He jumped. "Jeez, Rainey, I thought you were inside. You scared me."

She wasn't about to admit that he had scared her. "Do you have to hammer on the door like the Gestapo?"

The look of comprehension that flashed across his face made her feel he was reading her mind. Suddenly she became conscious of the basket of underwear. She didn't know which she hated worse, Blake's knowing about her father or having to stand there with a basket of underwear. She wished she could ditch the basket somewhere.

"So," he asked hesitantly, "how did, uh, everything go?"

"Okay."

A small dog of undefinable parentage was standing at the steps, barking. "Does that thing bite?"

"Well, it's never bitten me. It belongs to the neighbors."

"Look, we can't talk out here."

The Corvette, a blaze of sleek red, glistened in the sunshine. Blake had pulled it up directly in front of the steps. Rainey fancied people were looking out their windows at them. But she couldn't ask Blake in. The cotton sweater was spread out on a towel in the middle of the living room and the paper was littering the couch, as usual. Her father, the barking dog, the messy living room—suddenly it was too much for her to deal with. She could almost have burst into tears.

"Let's go for a ride," said Blake.

Stop reading my mind! she felt like saying. Go away. But she was hardly in a position to say any such thing when she owed him a hundred dollars.

"Okay." She put the basket down on the ground. She only hoped the stupid dog didn't run off with her underwear.

"Don't you think you'd better put that inside?" Blake looked uncertainly at the scraggly little dog.

Rainey flushed. "Just a minute." She inched past him and shoved the basket inside and slammed the door.

A minute later they were driving down the dusty road. The Corvette was as different from Rainey's vehicle as dragonflies are different from potatoes. It might have been a singing bird about to take flight. Rainey wondered if driving a car like it would make you feel like a different sort of person, not just richer, but freer and luckier and better-looking.

Blake looked at her. "So how did it go?"

"You already asked me that."

"Come on, Rainey. We're on the open road now. Nobody can hear us. We don't have to play games, do we? Did your father get off all right?"

"Yes." Her voice sounded muffled to her own ears as she watched the trees whiz by outside.

"I guess you don't want to talk about it."

"That's right." Rainey realized that she wanted to keep what she had of her father to herself. She didn't want to share him. She didn't want to talk about him and risk seeing him the way Blake saw him. Now that he was gone, her heart overflowed with warmth for him. She felt as sentimental as a Father's Day card. She knew the feeling would eventually pass, but since it was the closest thing she was likely to have to a normal family life, she wanted to enjoy it. "How did you find out about him? How did you know?"

"Jesse saw you back by the tobacco barn one morning and I just went to check out what was going on. Once I saw your father, well, I spotted the resemblance. Then when I passed you on the road that sort of cinched it."

She turned, intending to say something, but she forgot what it was. She hadn't noticed until then that Blake had a flesh-colored Band-Aid on his face. "You hurt yourself!"

Blake fingered his jaw. "Yeah."

"You shouldn't get into fights."

"Who told you I was in a fight? How do you know I didn't run into a door or something?"

"Tucker told me about it. He called a little while ago. Only I didn't realize he had landed a punch. I thought you had just hit him. Why did you do that, Blake?"

"He pushed me. What would you expect me to do? Grovel?"

"Well, he must have had some reason. He wouldn't just go and push you for no good reason."

"You're starting to make me mad. He had a good reason for hitting me, but I didn't have a good reason for hitting him? What are you saying? I just accidentally bumped against him and then he got nasty. He's a jerk. Be honest, Rainey, doesn't the guy get on your nerves?"

"No! You know he doesn't. I like him. We're going to the movies tonight. In fact, you're the first to know. I think I'm falling in love." She raised her chin defiantly.

"Oh, don't be stupid, Rainey, you don't love Tucker!"

She stiffened. "I'm not going to have you coming around here and telling me what I think and what I feel just because you lent me a hundred dollars, Blake Farraby."

"Forget the hundred dollars!"

"I can't."

"Do you think I'd have given it to you if I'd known it would make you mad at me?"

"I'm not mad at you."

"What do you call it, then?"

"I don't know." She closed her eyes. "I guess I am mad at you, but I don't know why. I wish you hadn't hit Tucker. I wish you hadn't said bad things about him. And I wish you hadn't given me that hundred dollars."

"Don't be mad at me, Rainey."

"It's been kind of tough for the past couple of weeks." She folded her hands in her lap and bit her lip.

"I know. But look, you and I, we're friends, aren't we?" He looked at her, but she didn't say anything. "All I'm saying is don't get the people who care about you mixed up with the people who are using you."

"How can you sit there and say that Tucker is using me? You have no reason in the world to say that. Honestly, I think you're just trying to rain on my parade."

"No. No, I'm not. Rainey, he goes through girls like gumdrops. Ask anybody. He's a collector."

"I'm not just any old girl, you know."

"I know that. I *know* that. Look, all I'm asking you is not to cross me off your list, okay?"

"I'm not crossing you off my list. I owe you a hundred dollars."

"Will you stop that! You know that's not what I mean."

"I guess I don't see what you mean."

"Just give me a chance. Don't get yourself paired off with Tucker for good. Maybe you'd like to go to a movie with me, sometime, or something. A picnic. Dinner. Just keep your options open, that's all.

"Are you into some sick charity-type thing, Blake?"

"Am I never going to hear the end of that blipping hundred dollars? I'm serious."

"I realize that I have a slight problem with that."

"Well, that's something."

"I'm going to really think about what you said."

"Good."

"Can I go home now?"

Blake turned the car around. "You aren't still mad at me, are you?"

"I'm not mad at you. I *like* you. I'm grateful to you."

"Scratch the grateful."

"Well, I can't help it. I am grateful. That was really nice of you to come up with the hundred dollars. Nobody else would have done that for me." She swallowed. "And I really am grateful."

"You're so grateful you're choking on it. Rainey, I don't want you walking out of my life and into Tucker's."

She smiled a little. "Not a chance."

"You promise me that?"

"Yes. I promise I'll keep my options open." She reached outside the window and patted the car. She liked the feel of the wind on her fingers. She was beginning to feel better. It had occurred to her that Blake was trying to tell her something and that she was too upset to really take it in. "I don't tell just anybody this," she said. "But I have a name for my car. I call it Old Betsy."

"I won't tell anybody."

"Do you have a name for your car?"

"I call it Happily Ever After."

"You don't!"

"It's the truth!"

He turned onto the dirt road and they drove up to Rainey's trailer. The scraggly little dog came out at once and began barking.

"I'm going to kill that dog," said Blake. "So, did you hear what I've been saying, Rainey?"

She nodded. "Mostly." She leaned over and kissed him. When she pulled away, he was smiling.

She awkwardly backed out of his car.

"I'll call you tonight."

She shook her head. "Tomorrow."

"Oh, right. Tucker, jeez, I hate him. Tomorrow. Is that a promise?"

"That's a promise."

The sunlight turned her hair to fire as she stood in front of the trailer, waving to him. Things were not quite as solid as Blake would have liked. Tucker was not, for example, stone-cold dead. But on the whole he felt good. He could almost believe in happily ever after.

To find out what happens next at West Mount High, look for *Senior Year at Last,* coming in May 1990.